THE HEALING WORD

2021 "The Healing Word"

Copyright © 2021 All rights reserved

ISBN 978-1-7377290-0-6

For more information on the content of this book,
email thecreativefaithconcepts@gmail.com

JMPinckney Publishing Company, LLC
104 Berkeley Square Lane
PMB 28
Goose Creek, South Carolina 29445

Cover Design:
Kathryn S. Jenkins

First printing August 2021 / Printed in the United States of America

Contents

Dedication

To my beloved wife Kathryn, who sees my desire, and whose love and support has motivated me to keep on keeping on, and to everyone who would DARE to believe, that: "If you have faith, Nothing Shall be impossible unto you."!

THE HEALING WORD

Disclaimer

The author of this book is not a medical doctor or practitioner. Following the advice or exercises in this book must be done at your discretion. It is not intended to replace personal medical care from a licensed health care practitioner.

***** Possible Scriptures ****

Mark 9:23 – If thou can'st believe. All things are possible to him who believes.

Preface

"No Condemnation, Nothing Incurable"

Handbook on Life, Living, Health and Healing

Throughout my childhood and until I was 30 years old, I had experienced 'UP' days and 'down' days. It seemed as if there were more 'down' days than up. What do I call down days? Well, there were either days when I felt sickly, or anxious, or fearful (I was extremely shy) or depressed, (even though most of the depression came after I was grown). I always wanted to do something great. I dreamed of becoming, yet it all seemed unreachable. And then one day when all of the depression, all of the ill feelings, all the anxieties and perplexities came to a 'head', by Divine Inspiration, I dropped down on my knees, in the middle of the day and cried out to the God I had heard about (but didn't know) and asked Him to "save me" "forgive me of my sins." When I did, something happened inside of me that made me to know that I would never be the same again. It was like a light turned on in my consciousness. All of a sudden I was introduced to the unseen world, the world of the Creator of heaven and earth, the sea, and all that therein is.

I came in contact with the world where 'all things are possible." And through years of study, worship, and experience in the supernatural, I am fully persuaded that through Jesus, (who is the Righteousness of God) and who is made unto us wisdom, righteousness, sanctification and redemption according to (1st Corinthians 1:30), and with God, there is therefore now no condemnation, Nothing INCURABLE.

This manual, along with your Bible is designed to take you through some proven steps to healing, deliverance, miracles, breakthroughs and Divine Life that only God can provide.

And He Has!
Rh Jenkins

Introduction

Hello, I'm Rh Jenkins

I would like to introduce you to a tremendously powerful way of being whole, well and enjoying good health. **3ʳᵈ John 2** says Beloved, I wish above all things that thou mayest prosper and be in Health, even as thy (your) soul prospereth. So that is my desire for you; that you prosper and be in good, vibrant, dynamic health. Regardless of what condition your health or body is in right now, whether you look and feel like the "Board of Health" or, are experiencing symptoms of sickness, disease or pain; or a long term illness or experiencing what the medical profession has termed an 'INCURABLE' condition. The good news I have for you today is that with God, all things are possible: Healing, Divine Health, FREEDOM, Deliverance, Miracles, whatever you need from God. Believe and Receive!

During a study on healing and health, a word from **Romans 8** stood out above the rest as I read **Romans 8:1**. That word was condemnation: There is therefore now, no condemnation to them which are in Christ Jesus, who walk not after the flesh, but after the spirit. When studying I like to define and research words, so immediately I went to my dictionary and references on the word 'condemnation': The word condemn, condemnation: Bring or pronounce against; judgment executed; unfit for use; to pronounce 'Incurable'. That came as a divine revelation to me that if we are in Christ Jesus, and as verse 2 gives us the condition for being Free: who walk (or live) Not after the flesh (after the five physical senses) but after the spirit. For the Law of the Spirit of Life in Christ Jesus hath made me free from the law of sin and death.

In these scriptures we see that there are two things necessary or required for one to receive this great promise of God.

1. First of all, a person must be "in" Christ Jesus

2. They must walk (or live) after the Spirit, or according to the Law or Word of God.

Both of these requirements are available to the entire human race. For the Word of God says in **John 3:16**, For God so loved the world that He gave His only begotten Son, That whosoever believeth in Him should not perish but have everlasting life.

1. What does it mean to be in 'Christ Jesus?'

1 Peter 1:23 – Being born again, not of corruptible seed, but of incorruptible, by the Word of God which liveth and abideth forever.

Being born again is the first requirement.

So how does one become born again?

Romans 10:9-10, 13 – That if thou shalt confess with thy mouth the Lord Jesus (or to say or confess Jesus is Lord) and shalt believe in thine heart that God hath raised Him from the dead, thou shalt be saved – For with the heart man believeth unto righteousness, and with the mouth confession is made unto salvation.

13 – For whosoever shall call on the name of the Lord shall be saved.

* Here is a sample prayer for salvation:

Heavenly Father,

I come to you in the name of Jesus,

It is written in your Word that whosoever shall call on the name of the Lord shall be saved, and that If I shall confess with my mouth that Jesus is Lord, and believe with my heart that God hath raised Him from the dead, I shall be saved. So I confess right now "Jesus is my Lord," And I believe in my heart that God has raised Him from the dead. Forgive me of my sins.

And now Father, fill me with your Holy Spirit, give me a language of prayer (Luke 11:13, Acts 2:4). Thank you Lord for coming into my heart and for giving me your Holy Spirit. In Jesus name – Amen

2nd Cor. 5:17 – Therefore if any man (woman, boy or girl) be in Christ, he is a new creature; old things have passed away, behold all things have become new.

Now that you are assured of the first requirement, let's look into the second.

2. You must walk in the Spirit.

Galatians 5:16 – This I say then, walk in the Spirit and ye shall not fulfill the lust of the flesh.

Galatians 5:22 – But, the fruit of the spirit is love, joy, peace, long suffering, gentleness, meekness, faith, goodness, temperance. Against such there is no Law!

So to walk in the spirit is to (live) walk in love, joy, peace, longsuffering, gentleness, goodness, faith, meekness and temperance.

We will be defining these fruit of the spirit and the two major laws of the spirit world (that governs everything in this natural world) in chapter one.

In my own "paraphrase" I would write **Romans 8:1** as saying, "There is therefore Now 'Nothing Incurable' to them which are in Christ Jesus, who walk not after the flesh, but after the spirit.

Nothing Incurable – Nothing Impossible -- Do you believe? Let's begin with the Two Major Laws.

Define Incurable:

Not able to be cured; untreatable.

*That which can only be cured from within.

CHAPTER ONE
The Two Major Laws

Romans 8:1-2 - There is therefore now *no condemnation to them

which are in Christ Jesus, who walk not after the flesh, but after the Spirit. For the law of the Spirit of life in Christ Jesus hath made me free from the law of sin and death. *NO condemnation: Nothing incurable; no judgment executed; no death sentence.

We see from this scripture that there are two major spiritual laws operating in this universe: The Law of the Spirit of Life, which is in Christ Jesus, and the Law of sin and death. So everything in the universe operates by Law and not by chance or luck. That means you can strike the word 'Luck' out of your vocabulary!

- To blame God for catastrophes, misfortune, death, sickness, disease or anything that would steal, kill or destroy is pure ignorance. In **Hosea 4:6,** God says, "My people are destroyed for lack of knowledge." So everything contrary or adverse to what you are believing for or expecting comes about as a result of a violated law. Laws are established by words, so words set in motion and activate these laws.

We understand that these laws are the complete opposite of one another and are enforced by two different forces, or spirit beings.

*First, let's look at the Law of sin and death and see how it operates:

The Works of the Flesh

Galatians 5:19 - Now the works of the flesh are manifest; which are these; adultery, fornication, uncleanness, lasciviousness, idolatry, witchcraft, hatred, variance, emulations, wrath, strifes, seditions, heresies, envying, murders, drunkenness, revellings and such like.

Examples of Such Likes: 1 Corinthians 6:9-10, 2 Corinthians 12:20, Mark 7:21, Rom. 1:29-31.

1 Corinthians 6:9-10 - Do you not know that the unrighteous shall not inherit the Kingdom of God? Be not deceived, neither fornicators, nor idolaters, nor adulterers, nor effeminate, nor abusers of themselves with mankind, nor thieves, nor covetous, nor drunkards, nor revilers, nor extortioners will inherit the kingdom of God.

Forces under the Law of sin and death:

The 'Such Likes':

Mark 7:21 - For from within, out of the heart of men proceed evil thoughts, adulteries, fornications, murders, thefts, covetousness, wickedness, deceit, lewdness, an evil eye, blasphemy, pride, foolishness.

Romans 1:29-32 - Being filled with all unrighteousness, fornication, wickedness, covetousness, maliciousness, full of envy, murder, strife, deceit, evil-mindedness, whisperers, backbiters, haters of God, violent, proud, boasters, inventors of evil things, disobedient to parents, undiscerning, untrustworthy, unloving, unforgiving, unmerciful, who – knowing the judgment of God, that those who practice (do) such things are deserving of death, not only do such things but have pleasure in those that do them.

2 Corinthians 12:20b - Lest there be contentions, jealousies, wrath, strife, backbitings, whispering, conceits, tumults.

NOTE:

Romans 1:32 - Those who do such things are deserving of death.

Romans 6:23 - for the wages of sin is death.

Defining the works of the flesh from Galatians 5:19

1. **Adultery** - unlawful sexual intercourse with the spouse of another person.

   Scripture: **Exodus 20:14** - Thou shalt not commit adultery.

2. **Fornication**: Illicit sexual intercourse on the part of an unmarried person.

   Scripture: **1 Thessalonians 4:3** - For this is the will of God, even your sanctification, that you should abstain from fornication.

3. **Uncleanness**: Impure, filthiness, morally or physically (unclean) impure.

   Scripture: **1 Thessalonians 4:7** - For God hath not called us to uncleanness, but unto holiness.

Examples of Uncleaness: cursing, foul language, indecent exposure, a mind full of lust or evil thoughts.

4. **Lasciviousness**: No restraint, excess, (dead to shame) shameless conduct, no self control.

    Scripture: **Jude 4** - There are certain men crept in unawares, ungodly men, turning the grace of God into lasciviousness. (these men did anything that came to their minds).

5. **Idolatry**: Worship of a made image or anything as a god (other than the Creator God), excessive love for anything that takes the place of God such as astrology, horoscope, statues, the sun, the moon, sacred animals, etc.

    Scripture: **Acts 17:16** - Now while Paul waited for them at Athens, his spirit was stirred in him when he saw the city wholly given to idolatry, (full of the images of the gods).

    Scripture: **Exodus 20:3-5** - Thou shalt have no other gods before me, thou shalt not make unto thee any graven image or any likeness of anything that is in heaven above or that is in the earth beneath or that is in the water under the earth. Thou shalt not bow down thyself to them nor serve them.

6. **Witchcraft** (sorcery): The word sorcery comes from the word pharmacy. Primarily signifies the use of medicine, drugs or spells to appeal to occult powers. The drugs were used to keep the applicants attention away from the power of demons and to impress them with the mysterious resources and powers of the sorcerer, witchdoctor, physic, etc.; the workings of demons through human individuals.

    Scripture: **Acts 8:9** - But there was a certain man called Simon, which before time in the same city used sorcery (magical arts, practiced witchcraft) and bewitched the people of Samaria, pretending to have some great power.

    Scripture:**Exodus 22:18** - Thou shalt not suffer a witch to live.

    Leviticus 20:27 - a man or woman with a familiar spirit, or a wizard shall be stoned to death.

7. **Hatred**: (bitterness) - a malicious or unjustifiable feeling towards others, animosity, ill will, often resentment, tending towards hostile action.

    Bitterness: to cut, to prick, a condition of extreme wickedness. Ongoing hatred: a root of bitterness.

    Scripture: **Proverbs 10:12** - Hatred stirreth up strifes, but love covers all sin.

    1 John 3:15 - Whosoever hateth his brother is a murderer, and you know that no murderer hath eternal life abiding in him.

8. **Variance**: To cut apart, to divide in two; discord, dissention, dispute, quarrel. A disagreement between two parts of the same legal proceeding, which in effectual (in order to be effective) ought to agree.

   Note: A major cause of church splits.

9. **Emulation**: To burn with jealousy, desire to have, an ambition or endeavor to equal or excel, the spirit of competition.

10. **Wrath**: anger, hot anger, passion, rage infuriate, enraged.

    Scripture: **Ephesians 4:31** - Let all bitterness, and anger, and wrath be put away from you with all malice.

11. **Strife**: disputes, arguments, fightings, earnest endeavor, contention for superiority, conflict, discord.

    Scripture: **2ⁿᵈ Timothy 2:24** - And the servant of the Lord must not strive, but be gentle, apt to teach, patient.

    James 3:16 - For where envy and strife is, there is confusion and every evil work.

12. **Seditions**: a standing apart, an insurrection, exciting discontent against authority (church or government).

    Scripture: **Numbers 16** - Korah led a rebellion against the leadership of Moses and God's authorized leadership.

Note: The Korah spirit will get into a church congregation and cause seditions, strifes etc. The Korah spirit will get into someone who doesn't agree with leadership and will cause them to influence others and then a rebellion is the outcome.

**A church I once attended had such a person who felt that the pastor should be 'replaced'. He talked about "impeaching the pastor," so he led a rebellion against authority and eventually he left. About a year later he was strickened with a severe heart attack and died*. It is a dangerous thing to rebel against God's delegated authority.

- One of the first thoughts that came to my mind, (after hearing of his passing) was "impeach the pastor."

13. **Heresies**: Differences of opinion, self willed opinion which is substituted for submission to the power of the truth and leads to division and the formation of sects.

    Scripture: **1 Corinthians 11:19** - For there must be heresies among you.

    Note: wonder why there are so many religious groups or sects?

14. **Envying**: The feeling of displeasure, produced by witnessing, or hearing of the advantage or prosperity of others.

- Envy desires to deprive another of what he has.

- Jealously desires to have the same or same sort of thing for himself.

  James 3:16b - For where envying and strife is, there is confusion and every evil work.

  Note: When envy is in operation, the very act of envying will cut that person off from ever receiving what they desire.

15. **Murderers**: One who unlawfully kill a human being with malice aforethought, express or implied to kill with premeditated malice.

  Scripture: **Matthew 15:19** - Out of the heart proceed evil thoughts, murders, adultery, etc.

  1 John 3:15 - Whosoever hateth his brother is a murderer; and ye know that no murderer hath eternal life abiding in him.

16. **Drunkenness**: Being in a state of mental intoxication, habitual intoxication, drenched, saturated (primarily referring to being intoxicated with alcoholic beverages, drugs, etc.)

  Note: (False teachers lead others to have a drunken spirit)

- Religion can make a person spiritually drunk.

  Scripture: **Ephesians 5:18-19** - And be not drunk with wine wherein is excess, but be filled with the Spirit, speaking to yourselves in psalms, hymns and spiritual songs, singing and making melody in your hearts to the Lord.

  Another definition of the word drunk is 'stupid' (or to be in a stupor or drunken state). Religion can make a person stupid!

17. **Revelling**: Partying - merrymaking, seeking pleasure constantly, sporting, to take great or intense delight in, satisfaction, merry or noisy celebration.

  And "Such Like" - of the which I tell you before as I have also told you in time past, that they which do such things shall not inherit the Kingdom of God.

- We want to inherit the Kingdom of God. To stay free from the Law of sin and death, we need to know how the kingdom of God operates. Now, in the Kingdom of God there is no sickness, no disease, no lack, no fear, no death, no poverty, no condemnation.

So to live, we need to know the Law of the Spirit of Life (And be free from the Law of sin and death).

Mark 4:14-32 - So is the Kingdom of God, as if a man should cast seed into the ground, and should sleep and rise night and day, and the seed should spring and grow up, he knoweth not how. For the earth bringeth forth fruit of herself, first the blade, then the ear, after that the full corn in the ear. But when the fruit is brought forth immediately he puttest in the sickle, because the harvest is come.

In **Luke 8:11** - Now the parable is this: The seed is the Word of God. Those by the wayside are they that hear, then cometh the devil and taketh away the word out of their hearts lest they should believe and be saved.

Note: This very important illustration of the Parable of the Sower shows how to receive anything from God. Comparing the natural planting of a seed into the ground and how that seed sprouts (springs up) and grows and produces whatever seed is sown in the ground, (whether corn, or wheat or whatever) the ground will produce whatever seed is planted into it). The spiritual side explains that the seed is the Word of God, and the ground is the heart or spirit of a person.

When the Word of God, the seed, is received (planted) into the spirit, (ground) of someone and allowed to grow, it will produce whatever that word describes. (i.e. "By whose stripes ye were healed," if stayed in the spirit long enough to take 'root' it will produce healing in that person's life.

Just as a farmer must watch over his crops to keep the birds out, to keep the weeds out, and to make sure it gets the proper amount of water, fertilizer etc., you must watch over the 'seed' or the word that's planted into your heart. You water it by continually confessing and hearing the Word. (Faith cometh! By hearing and hearing, continually, and faith is the substance, the manifestation of the thing you hope for). You fertilize your spiritual seed by constant thanksgiving and praise.

Proverbs 4:20-23 - My son, attend to my words; incline thine ear unto my sayings, let them (my words) not depart from thine eyes; keep them (my words) in the midst of thine heart, for they (my words) are life unto those that find them, and health to all their flesh. Keep thy heart with all diligence; for out of it flows the issues (forces) of life.

- Everything in your life is produced by your spirit, or heart. So you must protect your heart, watch what goes in there. Watch for fear, doubt, unbelief or anything contrary to the Word of God. These things will choke off or steal the word or 'seed' out of your heart.

Mark 4:14-25 - The sower soweth the word, and these are they by the wayside where the word is sown; but when they have heard, satan cometh immediately and taketh away the word that was sown in their hearts.

16. And these are they likewise which are sown on stony ground, who, when they have heard the word, immediately receive the word with gladness;

17. And have no root in themselves, and so endure but for a time: afterward when affliction or persecution ariseth for the word's sake, immediately they are offended.

18. And these are they which are sown among thorns; such as hear the word,

19. And the cares of this world, and the deceitfulness of riches, and the lust of other things entering in, choke the word, and it becometh unfruitful (did not produce the desired results)

20. And these are they which are sown on good ground, such as hear the word, and receive it, and bring forth fruit, some thirty fold, some sixty and some an hundred.

21. And he said unto them, is a candle brought to be put under a bushel, or under a bed and not to be set on a candlestick?

22. For there is nothing hid, which shall not be manifested; neither was anything kept secret, but that it should come abroad.

23. If any man have ears to hear, let him hear, and he said unto them,

24. Take heed what you hear: with what measure ye mete, it shall be measured to you: and unto you that hear shall more be given.

25. For he that hath, to him shall be given: and he that hath not, from him shall be taken even that which he hath.

- So this is how the kingdom operates: It's like a farmer planting seeds into the ground, and watching over his seed until it produces a crop or a harvest. The same way you plant, or have the seed (the word) planted into your heart (spirit) by hearing the preached word in person or on audio, and watching that word, you receive the word by agreeing with the word, and not allowing anything contrary to enter your heart you must realize that you have an enemy, who Jesus says in John 10:10 is a thief.

John 10:10 - the thief cometh not, but for to steal, and to kill, and to destroy: I am come that they might have Life, and have it more abundantly.

So who is this thief? This enemy?

1 Peter 5:8-9 - Be sober, be vigilant, because your adversary (opponent, enemy, foe) the devil, as a roaring lion, walkest about, seeking whom he may devour, whom resist steadfast in the faith, (stand against him with your faith!)

Ephesians 6:16 - above all, taking the shield of faith, wherewith ye shall be able to quench all the fiery darts of the wicked (devil.)

- What are these fiery darts that the enemy brings against you? We find them in Mark 4:17-19.

How the thief steals the Word

The fiery darts of the wicked - Mark 4:17-19 - Ephesians 6:16.

17. 1. Affliction

2. Persecution

19. 3. The cares of this world

4. The deceitfulness of riches

5. The lust of other things

You must guard your heart, and not allow these things to destroy the seed (The Word) planted in your heart.

1. **Affliction** - to suffer hardship, to be troubled due to the pressure of circumstances, antagonism of persons such as the enemy bringing thoughts to your mind: "you know that won't work" or "look at this or look at that, trying to get you to focus on the circumstances instead of what God is saying or having people tell you things contrary to the word, anything that would torment your mind or burden your Spirit.

2. **Persecution** - To put to flight, to drive away; pressure brought against you to get you to back off or turn back from the thing you are after, to pursue in a manner to injure, to cause to suffer because of belief, to harass or annoy with urgent attacks, pleas or the like.

- Persecution comes against you to cause you to back away from what you believe. If you back away, you don't get it. You must be persistent!

3. The Cares of this world

Cares -- anxieties, worries, mental suffering or grief, a burdensome sense of responsibility. Worry: troubling and engrossing emotion or affair, oppression of the mind, weighed down by responsibility or disquieted by apprehension.

Anxiety -- stresses, anguish or fear coupled with uncertainty or expectancy of misfortune.

Worry -- suggest fretting or stewing over problems, persons or situations that may or may not be a real cause of anxiety, (to get you sidetracked).

(Researchers have said that 92% of our worries are unnecessary and that the other 8% we have control over or can control.

Philippians 4:6-7 - Be careful for Nothing, but in everything by prayer and supplication with thanksgiving, let your request be known unto God and the peace of God which passeth all understanding shall keep your hearts and minds through Christ Jesus.

Be careful for nothing for Nothing, in other words, don't worry about a thing!

Matthew 6:25 - (Jesus said) Therefore I say unto you, take no thought for your life, what ye shall eat, or what ye shall drink, nor yet for your body, what ye shall put on.

Take no thought, the word 'thought' here means to be anxious or worried. He is saying there's more to life than food and clothes, and worrying about these things won't bring anything to you.

Matthew 6:33 - But seek ye first the kingdom of God, and His righteousness, and all these things shall be added unto you. Take therefore no thought for the morrow, for the morrow shall take thought for the things of itself.

1 Peter 5:7 - Casting all your care upon Him, for He careth for you.

Seek God's Kingdom and His righteousness. Seek God's way of doing things and your rights to operate in His kingdom.

(**Romans 8:17** - We are heirs of God and joint heirs with Jesus Christ. As a child of God, as an heir of God, you have a right to all that God has!)

- So, how do you operate the kingdom?

Mark 4:26-27 - So is the kingdom of God, as if a man should cast seed into the ground, and should sleep and rise night and day and the seed should spring and grow up, he knoweth not how. For the earth bringeth forth fruit of herself.

The earth here is referring to the heart, or the spirit of a person, the seed is the Word of God. According to Luke 8:11 – Now the parable is this: The seed is the word of God.

Matthew 13:19 - describes the word sown as being the Word of the Kingdom.

Matthew 13:19 - When anyone heareth the Word of the Kingdom, and understandeth it not, then cometh the wicked one and catcheth away that which was sown in his heart.

- So keep the cares, worries, anxieties and fears out of your heart by watching what goes in there. Newscast, newspaper and a constant hearing of negative talk and street talk will choke the word of God in your heart and will keep it from producing results in your life.

4. The Deceitfulness of Riches

Being deceived or lured after riches. Deceived of being under the false impressions that riches is the answer to your situation or being tricked into thinking that riches is a substitute and being pulled off your mission.

- Jesus was tempted in this way by the devil in Matthew chapter 4:1-11 and in Luke 4:1-14.

Matthew 4:8 - again, the devil taketh Him into an exceeding high mountain and showeth Him all kingdoms of the world, and the glory of them, (all the glamour) and saith unto Him, all these will I give thee, if thou wilt fall down and worship me. Then saith Jesus to him, get thee hence satan: for it is written, thou shalt worship the Lord thy God and Him only shalt thou serve.

Jesus knew his mission, and he wasn't about to be swayed by the glamour, the splendor, or the riches of this world, besides, satan's main purpose was to defeat Jesus' mission.

1 John 3:8 - He that commits sin is of the devil, for the devil sinneth from the beginning. For this purpose the Son of God was manifested, that He might destroy the works of the devil.

So, it pays to serve God, no matter how tempting these 'side' deals look.

*Examples of 'side deals':

1. Taking on a second, or third job that will draw you away from church services and devotional time, and family time.

2. Cheating or stealing on the job or using unjust means to succeed.

5. Lust of other things

When desire for things other than what you believe God for takes first place, it is time to take inventory. You can keep these things from entering in your heart by looking to the word day and night and by meditating, having a clear picture of what you want and doing everything you know to do to reach that goal. Have an expectant attitude and give glory to God. You must be fully persuaded that what God has promised, He is able also to perform.

Don't let the seed (the word) out of the ground (your spirit) until it produces the fruit (the thing you desire). If you allow these things:

1 – Afflictions - 2 – persecutions - 3 the cares of this world - 4 - the deceitfulness of riches - 5 - the lust of other things: to enter in, these forces will take the word out of your heart and you won't have your desired harvest.

Back to Luke 8:11 - Now the parable is this: The seed is the Word of God. Those by the way side are they that hear; then cometh the devil and taketh away the word out of their hearts, lest they should believe and be saved.

- The word 'saved' here is the key to your victory, because it means more than just having a 'ticket to heaven'.

The Bible's definition of the word "and be saved," could also be read: and be healed, "and delivered," "and be set free" (from anything: fear, lack, sickness, danger, defeat; anything that can steal, kill or destroy in your life!).

The Greek word for save, sozo - soteria - Define save, SAVED: of material and temporal deliverance from danger, suffering, etc. (to preserve) made whole; God's power to deliver from the bondage of sin; to bring safely through – escape; whole; guard or keep.

- Salvation, save and healing are from the same root - as saving from disease and its effect.

  SAVE: Health, safety, sound, whole.

  SAVE: - To avoid losing by being in time, (as long as you are breathing, you have hope.) to rescue from evil life; reclaim, also to redeem.

- To keep from being wasted or lost; preservation from destruction, failure or other evil.

- The idea of seeing: sin, sickness, poverty and death, destroyed.

James 5:14-15 - Is any sick among you? Let him call for the elders of the church, and let them pray over him, anointing him with oil in the name of the Lord, and the prayer of faith shall save the sick, and the Lord shall raise him up. -- The prayer of faith shall heal the sick.

- So we see that the word save or salvation have multiple meanings, and they all refer to your total freedom from the works of the devil, who Jesus says in **John 10:10** cometh to steal, kill and to destroy.

- Saved and Healed are used interchangeably in many scriptures.

Luke 18:35-43 - And it came to pass, that as he was come nigh unto Jericho, a certain blind man sat by the way side begging:

36. And hearing the multitude pass by, he asked what it meant,

37. And they told him, that Jesus of Nazareth passeth by.

38. And he cried, saying, Jesus, thou son of David, have mercy on me.

39. And they which went before rebuked him, that he should hold his peace: but he cried so much the more, Thou Son of David, have mercy on me.

40. And Jesus stood, and commanded him to be brought to him: And when he was come near, he asked him,

41. Saying, what wilt thou that I should do unto thee? And he said, Lord, that I may receive my sight.

42. And Jesus said unto him, receive thy sight: thy faith hath saved thee.

43. And immediately he received his sight and followed Him, glorifying

God: And all the people, when they saw it, gave praise unto God.

Notice - The blind man, had no doubt, heard of Jesus as being a healer, so he cried out to Jesus for mercy. Verse 42 – Jesus said unto him, receive thy sight, thy faith hath saved thee. Here again the words, thy faith hath saved thee can be translated, thy faith hath healed thee.

- We see here that Faith plays a very important part in receiving from God, and that faith can cause the impossible to become possible. Faith makes the incurable, curable.

- There is nothing that faith cannot cure!

- There is not anything that faith will not cure – Faith in God's word will always work.

- Faith is life's energy!

- The just shall live by faith. Gal 3:11, Heb 10:38, Rom. 1:17, Hab. 2:4

The Law of The Spirit of Life in Christ Jesus

The Word is the Cure

Ps. 107:20 - He sent his Word and healed them.

John 6:63 - It is the Spirit that quickeneth; the flesh profiteth nothing, the words that I speak unto you, they are spirit and they are life.

Proverbs 4:20-22 - My son, attend to my words; incline thine ear unto my saying, let them not depart from thine eyes, keep them in the midst of thine heart, for they (my words) are life unto those that find them, and health to all their flesh. Keep thy heart with all diligence, for out of it are the issues of life.

- God's word is medicine to all our flesh. That means that there is not anything God's word won't cure! There is not anything God's word cannot cure! If you've got the word, you've got the cure!

- Notice in vs. 23 – Keep thy heart with all diligence, for out of it are the forces of life.

We 'must' guard our hearts (spirits) with utmost care. Watch what you hear and see, (remember the Parable of the Sower – Mark 4:14). Negative words of death, debt, fear, lack, unbelief, cares, etc., will produce an overloaded spirit, which will adversely affect your mind and your body. "Take heed what you hear!" You don't need a steady stream of bad news going into your spirit!

- Everything has got a cure! **Mark 4:22** - For there is nothing hid, but it shall be manifested.

Galatians 3:13 - Christ hath redeemed us from the curse of the Law being made a curse for us.

According to **Deuteronomy 28:15-68**; every sickness and every disease is a curse of the law.

- To combat the Laws of sin and death (which causes sin, sickness, disease, poverty, death, fear, etc.) you need life giving forces, or the forces of life in your spirit.

Galatians 5:22 - List the fruit of the Spirit as the forces of life and states that, against these forces there is NO Law (verse 23).

When you are walking under the Law of love, joy, peace, longsuffering (patience), gentleness, goodness, faith, meekness, temperance, there is nothing that the law of sin and death can do against you!

- **Lets Define and Look into these Life giving Forces**

1. **Love**: Mercy, compassion, all giving, all sacrificing, (for God so loved, that he gave) John 3:16. God is Love. Love is being like God: merciful and compassionate.

The Fruit of the Spirit

Love

Let's look at some of the great qualities of love:

- Love is lasting - Love is willing to stay with you – patient, longsuffering.
- Love is Kind - tenderhearted, gracious.
- Love is never envious - never spiteful or grudging of what someone else has.
- Love is not jealous - mistrusting or suspicious or trying to impress.
- Love does not brag or exaggerates.
- Love is not full of pride - an over high opinion of oneself.
- Love is not puffed up - arrogant, overbearing.
- Love is not scornful - putting down others.
- Love is not rude - impolite, harsh, ill-mannered.
- Love is not dishonest or improper.
- Love does not call attention to himself.
- Love is not selfish.
- Love is not over-sensitive, nervous, irritable, easily offended, worried, vexed, annoyed, disturbed, agitated, resentful, easily insulted, takes no account of the evil done to it.
- Love is quick to forgive - love forgives and forgets.
- Love does not rejoice in wrongful acts.
- Love rejoices in what is right.

- Love tolerates, or puts up with anything - love knows how to deal with things.

- Love always believe the best about a person - Love turns off gossip.

- Love's hopes are always high, regardless of the circumstances. (Love knows - if I stay in love, "I'm backed by God!").

- Love endures everything - Never gives up, never lets down.

- Love never fails - love goes on forever, never comes to an end, never weakens, never decays.

- Love is never lacking - love doesn't have any needs, love is fulfilled in itself.

- Love is fearless - 1st John 4:18 - There is no fear in love; but perfect love casteth out fear, for fear has torment. He that feareth is not made perfect in love.

- Love cannot be defeated and Love Never Quits

- We can clearly see that love is the cure of all human ills!

- Why aren't more people walking, or living in this kind of love? Because of pressure from the enemy.

- Love is the greatest weapon you can find in any world: spiritual, mental, physical, financial, social - It Never Fails!

2. **Joy** - delight, gladness, expectation of good, experiencing good, pleasure, an agreeable feeling when what is desired is manifested; to satisfy. **As a child of God, you should expect the best!

NOTE: There is a difference between happiness and joy, happiness depends on the five physical senses, seeing, hearing, tasting, smelling, feeling, but joy is an inside force that doesn't depend on the natural. Joy is of the heart (spirit).

Nehemiah 8:10 - For the joy of the Lord is your strength.

Synonyms of Joy: rejoice, glad

Antonym of Joy: Pride. Pride is a counterfeit of joy.

3. **Peace** - harmony, harmonious relationships, friendliness, quietness, calm, reconcile, to make amends, freedom from fears, conflicts, aggravation. **Righteousness produces peace – knowing you have rights with God. Nothing missing, Nothing broken, Nothing lacking in your life:

Isaiah 32:17 - And the work of righteousness shall be peace; and the effect of righteousness, quietness and assurance forever.

Isaiah 26:3 - Thou wilt keep him in perfect peace, whose mind is stayed on thee: because he trusteth in thee.

- As faith comes by hearing the word of God, so peace comes by hearing the word of God. All nine fruit have an assignment and they work together. Without peace your faith is hindered.

4. Longsuffering - forbearance, patience, long tempered, endurance, perseverance. Endurance: to last, to continue without being overcome, to continue without perishing, persistent, steadfast pursuit of a goal, to persist in any endeavor in spite of contrary circumstances or opposition, (until it is accomplished).

Longsuffering is that quality of self restraint in the face of provocation. It is the opposite of anger.

Patient - bearing or enduring trials, temptations, etc., without complaining, undisturbed by obstacles, delays, failures.

Patience is the quality that does not surrender to circumstances or succumb under trial, it is the opposite of despondency, not being moved by what you hear, what you feel or what you see. Patience is the power to hold yourself calm. Patience is directly related to hope. (You persist long enough, you will begin to see more and more of your total victory. Patience is not waiting for something to happen, it is calmly seeing the obstacle removed by your faith! Patience works with your faith.

4. Longsuffering - (Scriptures)

2 Peter 3:9 - The Lord is not slack concerning His promise as some men count slackness; but is long-suffering to us-ward. Not willing that any should perish; but that all should come to repentance.

Luke 21:19 - In your patience possess ye your souls.

(You control your soul: your mind, your will and your emotions with patience.)* Patience keeps you from giving up!

5. Gentleness - Gentleness is being undisturbed in uncomfortable surroundings, not contentious, a quality of the wisdom from above, 'mild' mannered, as a 'gentleman'.

2 Timothy 3:24 - And the servant of the Lord must not strive (be contentious), but be gentle unto all men, apt to teach, patient.

James 3:17 - But the wisdom that is from above is first pure, then peaceable, gentle, easy to be entreated (easy to deal with) full of mercy and good fruits without partiality and without hypocrisy.

6. Goodness - Goodness is showing kindness, moral quality, being morally honorable, pleasing to God, upright, to bestow a benefit, to do good to and for others, disposed to promote the prosperity of others, in right standing, benevolent.

NOTE: The best way to get your needs met is to help others get their needs met.

Ephesians 6:8 - Knowing that whatsoever good thing any man doeth, the same shall he receive of the Lord.

Psalm 23:6 - Surely goodness and mercy shall follow me all the days of my life: And I will dwell in the house of the Lord forever.

7. Faith - Faithfulness

Faith: primarily, firm persuasions, a conviction based upon hearing. (Romans 10:17 – Faith cometh by hearing) to persuade, trust, assurance, a firm conviction based upon accepting Gods word as truth.

Hebrew 11:1 - Now faith is the substance of things hoped for, the evidence of things not seen.

Note: (For more on Faith, see Chapter 5 – A Positive Faith Attitude).

Faithfulness - loyal and dedicated to a person or a cause, trustworthy, true in affection, promise, allegiance, devoted.

Psalm 89:24 - But my faithfulness and my mercy shall be with him.

Matthew 25:21 - His Lord said unto him: Well done thou good and faithful servant: thou hast been faithful over a few things, I will make thee ruler over many things, enter thou into the joy of thy Lord.

8. Meekness - Accepting God's dealing with us as good, without disputing, challenging or resisting, condescending, not self centered, a mild temper, humility, a fruit of power, humble, a gentle disposition.

Matthew 5:5 - Blessed are the meek; for they shall inherit the earth.

1 Peter 5:6-7 - Humble yourselves therefore under the mighty hand of God, that He may exalt you in due time, casting all your care upon Him, for He careth for you.

Ephesians 4:2 - Walk worthy of the vocation wherewith you are called, with all lowliness and meekness, with longsuffering, forbearing one another in love.

9. Temperance - Temperance is self-control, the ability to control one's actions or habits. The practice of controlling one's appetites, passions or habits by an inner quality or force, not over indulging or excessive, being able to abstain or restrain.

1 Corinthians 9:25 - And every man that striveth for the mastery is temperate in all things.

Titus 1:8 - A bishop must be a lover of hospitality, a lover of good men, sober, just, holy, temperate in all things.

2 Peter 1:5-11 - And besides this giving all diligence, add to your faith virtue, and to virtue, knowledge, and to knowledge, temperance, and to temperance, patience, and to patience godliness, and to godliness, brotherly kindness, and to brotherly kindness, charity (love). For if these things be in you, and abound, they make you that ye shall neither be barren or unfruitful in the knowledge of our Lord Jesus Christ. But he that lacketh these things is blind, and cannot see afar off and hath forgotten that he was purged from his old sins. Wherefore the rather brethren, give diligence to make your calling and election sure: For if ye do these things, ye shall never fall: For so on entrance shall be ministered unto you abundantly into the everlasting kingdom of our Lord and Saviour Jesus Christ.

Galatians 5:23 - Against such (the fruit of the spirit) there is NO LAW.

There is no law that can stand against any of these fruit. No law that can defeat the fruit of the spirit. *When you have these fruit, these qualities (love, joy, peace, longsuffering (patience), gentleness, goodness, faith, meekness, temperance operating in your life, there is nothing satan can do, nothing the world can do or nothing the law of sin and death can do to defeat you. Nothing can steal, kill or destroy in your life!

For the Law of the Spirit of Life in Christ Jesus has made me free from the Law of sin and death.

Remember that everything in this universe operates by law, and not by luck or chance. What you sow is what you will reap.

- Love is the royal Law, the Supreme Law, and all the other fruits are qualities of love. Just as the human body needs certain vitamins for the many different organs and functions of the body, so your spirit need these fruit ("spiritual vitamins") to function at peak performance. So develop, practice, these life giving forces by: 1. Giving the word first priority in your life, 2. meditate (play a mental movie in your mind of this quality being a part of you, 3. act – (practice the word, do what the word describes), 4. live by faith (be assured of these fruits producing in your life), 5. make the decision to live the love life – Be FREE!

CHAPTER TWO
Defining Redemption

Applying the Principles

Galatians 3:13-14; 29 - Christ hath redeemed us from the curse of the law being made a curse for us, for it is written, cursed is everyone that hangeth on a tree: That the blessing of Abraham might come on the gentiles through Jesus Christ; that we might receive the promise of the Spirit through faith.

And if ye be Christ's, then are ye Abraham's seed and heirs according to the promise.

Define Redeem, Redemption - To buy. To buy out or to buy back especially of purchasing a slave, in view of his freedom, To Ransom (when we think of the word ransom we think of a price paid to free someone who has been kidnapped). Through Adam's treason, he allowed the devil to kidnap (so to speak) the whole human race from under God's care, and into his domain where he ruled over the earth with spiritual death, (which means to be separated from God), fear, poverty, sickness and disease. All of these things came into the world as a result of Adam's sin and his connection with satan, God's enemy.

Redeem - Redemption - To regain possession of by repurchase. To deliver from the bondage of sin and the penalties of God's violated law. Reclaim deliverance from the bondage and consequences of sin, as through Christ's atonement.

- Sickness and disease came about as the result of sin, (which brought the curse in the earth).

God found Himself in an unusual position: His man Adam, and the whole human family, along with the whole earth are now in the hands of God's enemy. A sinless man gave the earth, and his dominion over earth, to satan.

Now, *to be legal, it would take a sinless man to recapture the lost race of man, and the earth. *(God does everything by Law), but God had a plan: **John 3:16-17** - For God so loved the world, that He gave his only begotten Son, that whosoever believeth in Him should not perish but have everlasting life, for God sent not His Son unto the world to condemn the world; But that the world through him might be saved. So God, through making a covenant with Abraham made a way for His Son Jesus to come into the earth, and to pay the ransom price to free mankind from the doom (punishment,) of sin.

Romans 6:23 - For the wages (doom, penalty) of sin is death; but the gift of God is eternal life through Jesus Christ our Lord.

Jesus came into this earth and took upon himself the penalty of sin: (sickness, disease, fear, poverty and death) so that we can go free.

Isaiah 53:4-5 - Surely, he hath borne our griefs, and carried our sorrows (literal Hebrew: Surely he has lifted, carried or borne our sicknesses or diseases and our pains) yet we did esteem him stricken, smitten of God and afflicted, But, He was wounded for our transgressions, He was bruised for our iniquities; the chastisement of our peace was upon Him; and with his stripes we are healed.

- **Redeemed From Sickness, Poverty and Spiritual Death**

Galatians 3:13 - Christ hath redeemed us from the curse of the Law, being made a curse for us.

As we mentioned earlier, that Adam's disobedience to God, brought a curse upon the earth. The penalty for breaking the Law brought a threefold curse: sickness, poverty and spiritual death.

Everything that can cause failure in man is listed in the 28th chapter of Deuteronomy.

Verses 1-14 list the blessings that would come upon the people for obeying God's laws, verses 15-68 tell of the various curses that were to come upon them if they disobeyed.

Redeemed From Sickness

Deuteronomy 28:15 - But it shall come to pass, if thou wilt not hearken unto the voice of the Lord thy God, to observe to do all his commandments and his statutes which I command thee this day; that all these curses shall come upon thee, and overtake thee:

- Let's take a look at the definition of a curse: evil brought against, an invocation for harm or injury to come upon someone, to bring destruction or doom.

Verses:

16. cursed shalt thou be in the city, and cursed shalt thou be in the field.
17. cursed shalt be thy basket and thy store.

18.   cursed shall be the fruit of thy body and the fruit of thy land, the increase of thy kine and the flocks of thy sheep.

19.   cursed shalt thou be when thou cometh in, and cursed shalt thou be when thou goeth out.

20.   The Lord shall send upon thee cursing, vexation and rebuke in all that thou settest thine hand unto for to do, until thou be destroyed, and until thou perish quickly; because of the wickedness of thy doings, whereby thou hast forsaken me.

21.   The Lord shall make the pestilence cleave unto thee until he have consumed thee from off the land whither thou goest to possess it.

22.   The Lord shall smite thee with a consumption and with a fever, and with an inflammation, and with an extreme burning and with the sword and with blasting and with mildew; and they shall pursue thee until thou perish.

27.   The Lord shall smite thee with the botch of Egypt, and with the emerods, and with the scab, and with the itch whereof thou canst not be healed.

28.   The Lord shall smite thee with madness, and blindness and astonishment of heart:

29.   And thou shalt grope at noonday, as the blind gropeth in darkness and thou shalt not prosper in thy ways: and thou shalt be only oppressed and spoiled evermore, and no man shall save thee, ---

Deuteronomy 28:35 - The Lord shall smite thee in the knees, and in the legs with a sore botch that cannot be healed, from the top of thy head, to the soles of thy feet.

58.   If thou wilt not observe to do all the words of this Law that are written in this book, that thou mayest fear this glorious and fearful name, THE LORD THY GOD;

59.   Then the Lord will make thy plagues wonderful, and the plagues of thy seed even great plagues and of long continuance, and sore sicknesses and of long continuance.

60.   More over he will bring upon thee all the diseases of Egypt, which thou was afraid of; and they shall cleave unto thee.

61.   Also every sickness and every plague, which is not written in the book of this Law, them will the Lord bring upon thee, until thou be destroyed.

- Every sickness, every disease is a curse of the Law. Christ hath redeemed us from the curse of the law, being made a curse for us.

Note: The phrase "the Lord shall smite thee" seems to indicate that God is the one putting sickness and disease upon the people, But Bible scholars indicate that translations were done in the causative sense (implying that God is the cause) instead of the permissive sense, (indicating God permitted it). We must realize that the curse was already out there, God was only telling them what would happen if they transgress, or step out from under his protection. We notice in Deut. 28:1-14 that as long as Israel obeyed God, they were blessed and protected from all harm. When they disobeyed God, they stepped out from safety, into enemy territory.

A better translation should read "The Lord will allow these…to come upon thee." We must know that there was a thief in the earth, since Adam's day, and is still in the earth today.

John 10:10 - (Jesus said) The thief cometh not, but for to steal, and to kill, and to destroy: I am come that they might have life, and that they might have it more abundantly. And He is the same yesterday, today, and forever

Hebrews 13:8. God is not the thief!

- God is not our problem! He is our solution, our healer, Exodus 15:26 – "I am the Lord that healeth thee" He is our Redeemer, our deliverer, our provider, our protector, our saviour: "Who forgiveth all thine iniquities who healeth all our diseases." Psalm 103:3.

- In Deuteronomy 28:15-61 – A number of sicknesses and diseases are listed as being under the curse of the Law, and then verse 61 makes it all inclusive:

- Also every sickness and every plague which is not written in the book of this Law, them will the Lord bring upon thee until thou be destroyed." That means that every sickness and every disease is under the curse of the Law.

Matthews 9:35 - And Jesus went about all the cities and villages teaching in their synagogues, and preaching the gospel of the kingdom and healing every sickness and every disease among the people.

We can conclude that every sickness and every disease is a curse of the Law.

Let's go back to Galatians 3:13 - Christ hath redeemed us from the curse of the Law, being made a curse for us. So we have been redeemed from every sickness and every disease.

- Here's an exercise or confession that I believe will be of great help to you if done on a constant, continual basis until this truth takes hold of your consciousness and produce the results of healing in your body.

(Remember, these activities must be done at your discretion if you are under the care of a physician or health practitioner. If you are under medication, you don't have to discontinue your medication to do this exercise.)

Deuteronomy 28:15-68 - states that every sickness and every disease is a curse of the Law.

Galatians 3:13 - (says) Christ hath redeemed us from the curse of the law, being made a curse for us. *(Christ purchased our freedom from the curse of the law).

- Whatever sickness or disease that's in your body - for instance - Deuteronomy 28:27 - the Lord shall smite thee with the botch of Egypt, and with the emerods, and with the scab, 'Scab' means every form of skin disease. If you have skin disease on your body you can say:

"According to Deuteronomy 28:27, skin disease or 'scab' is under the curse of the Law, and according to Galatians 3:13, Christ has redeemed me from the curse of the Law, therefore I'm redeemed from skin disease."

You can be more specific if you know the exact name of that skin disease (ie eczema) - say "Eczema is a curse of the Law, Christ has redeemed me from the curse of the Law, therefore I no longer have eczema", "I'm redeemed". What ever the sickness or disease is called.

"According to Deuteronomy 28:61 - every sickness and every disease is a curse of the Law. (Name the condition) is a curse of the law, Christ has redeemed me from the curse of the Law, therefore I'm redeemed from _____." *I encourage you to write out your confession on a 3x5 card and confess and look at it day and night!

Galatians 3:13-14 - Christ hath redeemed us from the curse of the Law, being made a curse for us: For it is written, cursed is everyone that hangeth on a tree: That the blessing of Abraham might come on the gentiles through Jesus Christ; that we might receive the promise of the Spirit through faith.

- God made Adam, the first man, put him in the Garden of Eden, to dress and to keep it, and gave Adam instructions of things to do in the garden and ONE thing not to do:

Genesis 2:7 - But of the tree of the knowledge of good and evil, thou shalt not eat of it: for in the day that thou eatest thereof thou shall surely die.

Well, as the scripture tells us in Genesis 3: - Adam and Eve did what God told them not to do, and died, But notice that they didn't die physically at that moment, "But in the day that thou eatest thereof thou shalt surely die". They died spiritually. (Man is a spirit, he has a soul, and he lives in a physical body). It was some 930 years after Adam sinned, that he died physically.

There are three kinds of death:

1. Physical death: is what we know as natural death, where the spirit and the soul leave the body - James 2:26.

2. Spiritual death: means being separated from God, spirit to spirit connection is cut off.

3. Eternal death: forever separated from God, confined to a place called hell, the second death, thrown into a lake of fire.

- When Adam sinned and died spiritually, he was no longer a son or child of God; he yielded to the devil and became a child of the devil. To be reunited with God, mankind has to be born-again, this is a spiritual birth where God recreates the dead spirit of a person and makes him a new creature in Christ Jesus.

2 Corinthians 5:17 - Therefore if any man be in Christ, he is a new creature: old things are passed away; behold all things are become new.

- All things become new: spiritually, you still have your same body when you are born-again, but everything spiritually: your sins, old nature, are passed away. Remember too, that your mind is not new or recreated, you still have the same mind. Romans 12:2, Ephesians 4:23, James 1:21 tell us what to do to renew our minds.

Romans 12:2 - And be not conformed to this world; but, be ye transformed by the renewing of your mind, that ye may prove what is that good, and acceptable, and perfect, will of God.

Ephesians 4:23 - And be renewed in the spirit of your mind.

James 1:21 - Wherefore lay apart all filthiness and superfluity of naughtiness and receive with meekness the engrafted word, which is able to save your souls. (Your soul consists of your mind, will and emotions.)

Death is an enemy of God and man.

1 Corinthians 15:26 - The last enemy that shall be destroyed is death.

Understanding our Covenant with God

"A Covenant of Life"

To receive all that God has provided for, or promised to us, we must be aware of, and understand our covenant with God. When you accepted Jesus as your Lord and your Saviour, you entered into a covenant with Almighty God.

*What is a Covenant?

A covenant is solemn promise made binding by an oath. A 'coming together' of two (or more) parties, in which, both parties agree to and binds himself to the terms of the agreement or to fulfill certain obligations.

*In the Old Testament the Hebrew word 'berith' is always thus translated "to cut". A covenant is a cutting or dividing of animals into two parts and the contracting parties passing between them, making a covenant.

God's Covenant with Abraham

Genesis 15:1-18 - After these things the Word of the Lord came unto Abram in a vision, saying, fear not Abram: I am thy shield, and thy exceeding great reward.

2. And Abram said, Lord God, what wilt thou give me, seeing I go childless, and the steward of my house is this Eliezer of Damascus?

3. And Abram said, Behold, to me thou hast given no seed: and lo, one born in my house is mine heir.

4. And, behold, the word of the Lord came unto him, saying, this shall not be thine heir; but he that will come forth out of thine own bowels (body) shall be thine heir.

5. And He brought him forth abroad, and said, look now toward heaven, and tell the stars, if thou be able to number them: And he said unto him, so shall thy seed be.

6. And he believed in the Lord; and he counted it to him for righteousness,

7. And He said, I am the Lord that brought thee out of UR of the Chaldees, to give thee this land to inherit it.

8. And he said, Lord God, whereby shall I know that I shall inherit it?

9. And He said unto him, take me an heifer of three years old, and a she goat of three years old, and a ram of three years old, and a turtledove and a young pigeon.

10. And he took him all these, and divided them in the midst, and laid each piece one against another: but the birds divided he not.

11. And when the fowls came down upon the carcasses, Abram drove them away.

12. And when the sun was going down, a deep sleep fell upon Abram; and lo a horror of great darkness fell upon him.

13. And He said unto Abram, know of a surety that thy seed shall be a stranger in a land that is not theirs, and shall serve them; and they shall afflict them four hundred years;

14. And also that nation, whom they shall serve, will I judge: and afterwards they shall come out with great substance.

15. And thou shalt go to thy fathers in peace; thou shalt be buried in a good old age.

16. But in the fourth generation they shall come hither again for the iniquity of the Amorites is not yet full.

17. And it came to pass that, when the sun was down, and it was dark, behold a smoking furnace, and a burning lamp that passed between those pieces.

18. In the same day the Lord made a covenant with Abram saying, unto thy seed* have I given this land, from the river of Egypt, unto the great river, the river Euphrates;

Galatians 3:16 - Now to Abraham and his seed were the promises made. He saith not, and to seeds, as of many (plural); but as of one, and to thy seed, which is Christ.

The covenant God made with Abraham was to Abraham and his seed. **Galatians 3:16 - tells us that seed was Christ.

Galatians 3:29 - And if ye be Christ, then are ye Abraham' seed and heirs according to the promise.

Deuteronomy 28:15-68 - are listed every sickness, and every disease (plague) known or unknown to mankind vs. 61, also every sickness and every plague not written in the book of this law them will the Lord bring upon thee, until thou be destroyed.

Every calamity - Every diabolical (evil) thing that can cause failure to the human race: Poverty, sickness, disease, mental illnesses, blindness, confusion, drought, flood, war, defeat, robbery, lack, wayward children, weariness, fear, etc. Jesus came into the earth, shed His blood, ratifying the covenant God made with Abraham and his seed (which was Christ!)

He came to set us free from all these evil things.

Galatians 3:13-14 - Christ hath redeemed us from the curse of the Law, being made a curse for us, for it is written cursed is everyone that hangeth on a tree: That the blessing of Abraham might come on the gentiles through Jesus Christ; that we might receive the promise of the spirit through faith.

We are redeemed from every curse listed in Deuteronomy 28:15-68.

- Being Abraham's seed, (because of Christ) we have a covenant right to be free from every sickness and every disease: curable or incurable.

Deuteronomy 28:35 - a sore 'botch' (boil) that cannot be healed (incurable)

Deuteronomy 28:59 tells of plagues that are of long continuance and sore sickness that are of long continuance (incurable)

Galatians 3:14b - That we might receive the promise of the Spirit through faith.

*Faith is an important factor in receiving from God.

Hebrews 11:6 - But without faith, it is impossible to please Him (God), for he that cometh to God must believe that He is, and that He is a rewarder of them that diligently seek Him.

Psalm 89:34 - My covenant will I not break, nor alter the thing that is gone out of my lips.

Hebrews 6:13-15 - For when God made promise (covenant) to Abraham, because He could swear by no greater, He sware by himself saying, Surely blessing I will bless thee and multiplying I will multiply thee.

Hebrews 6:13-15 - **(v15)** and so, after he had patiently endured, he obtained the promise.

- The words "He sware by himself", meant that there was no higher power for God to sware by, meaning He put His whole existence on the line: meaning, "If I don't keep my part of the covenant, I will have to destroy myself." THAT is STRONG!!! And it is still real today!

The Name of Jesus

- As a Covenant child of God we have a right to use the Name of Jesus, (the name that is above every (all) names. Philippians 2:9-11.

By using the name of Jesus (in faith), you are making covenant demands as if Jesus himself were making them!

- Two ways to use the Name:
1. Pray to the Father in Jesus' Name.
2. Speak the name - making demands or using commands.

Example:

- In Jesus' name, I command you headache to leave!

In Jesus name, I give and it's given unto me, good measure shaken together and running over.

Philippians 2:9-11 - Wherefore God also hath highly exalted Him, and given him a name which is above every name: That at the name of Jesus every knee should bow, of things (beings) in heaven, and things (beings) in earth, and things (beings) under the earth, and that every tongue should confess that JESUS CHRIST IS LORD, to the glory of God the Father.

- The name of Jesus is above every name. Every sickness has a name, every disease has a name, even if it is just 'sickness' or 'disease'. The name of Jesus is above (over, higher than, superior in rank or power, beyond, surpassing) sickness and disease. That means that the name of Jesus is a higher power than sickness and disease, and when the name is applied, in faith, sickness and disease must bow (submit or yield) to that name!

The name of Jesus is above Cancer. The name of Jesus is above AIDS. The name of Jesus is above Lupus, Crohn's Disease, Alzheimers, Parkinson, Meningitis, Diabetes, high blood pressure, addiction, allergy, *above boils, anemia, aneurysm, apnea, asthma, bacteria, coma, constipation, dementia, depression, dermatitis, eczema, fibroids, fungus, gangrene, goiter, sores, hemorrhage, hemorrhoid, hernia, hives, infection, inflammation, palsy, phobias, plague, itch, rash, sclerosis, seizures, sinusitis, stroke, tumor, pain, virus, every sickness, every disease. And above every name that is named.

Ephesians 1:21 - Jesus is, far above all principality, and power and might and dominion and every name that is named.

Proverbs 18:10 - The name of the Lord is a strong tower, the righteous runneth into it, and is safe.

Think of the name of Jesus as a safe haven, or as a place of security you can run to when you face dangers or obstacles.

The Name of Jesus means "Savior". A call on that name will save you from all evil; however you must have faith in that name and know the authority that's in the name.

Ephesians 1:17-23 - That the God of our Lord Jesus Christ, the father of glory, may give unto you the spirit of wisdom and revelation in the knowledge of Him: The eyes of your understanding being enlightened; that ye may know what is the hope of his calling, and what the riches of the glory of his inheritance in the saints, And what is the exceeding greatness of his power to us-ward who believe, according to the working of his mighty power, Which he wrought in Christ, when He raised him from the dead, and set him at his own right hand in the heavenly places, Far above all principality, and power, and might, and dominion, and every name that is named, not only in this world, but also in that which is to come: And hath put all things under his feet, and gave him to be the head over all things to the church, which is His body, the fullness of him that filleth all in all.

Vs. 19 - says, "And what is the exceeding greatness of his power to us-ward who believe".

- **Note:** That power is in His Name, and it is far above all principality and power, and might and dominion, and every name that is named. The Name of Jesus is above all evil spirits. Jesus is the head of the church. We are the body of Christ, and all things have been put under His [Jesus] feet: evil spirits, sickness, disease, fear, poverty, death, every name that is named – We, being the body of Christ must realize that all these things are under our feet!

Personal Testimony: I remember growing up with several fears, among them, fear of death or even hearing of someone who had died, and how

those fears use to haunt me, and then there were fears of rejections, fear of failure, (once that conquered, the fear of success would try to take place). One night I went out and left my door unlocked and when I came back, this harassing fear that someone had sneaked into my house had me looking all over the place: This 'voice' saying "check the closets," Look under the bed", "Look in there". Then I thought to myself, "This doesn't make sense!" Well, one morning I turned on my radio to listen to Christian programs, the first thing I heard was "You've Got A Right To Use The Name Of Jesus! That phrase set me free! Somehow I knew there was power in the name, and when satan came back blowing his smoke of fear at me, I said: In the Name of JESUS!! I sensed I had 'hit' him (satan) where it hurts! You see, fear is a spirit. All fears are connected to the fear of death.

Important facts about the Name

2 Timothy 1:7 - For God hath not given us the spirit of fear; but of power, and of love, and of a sound mind. Whenever any kind of fear comes against your mind, rebuke it just as you are talking to a personality: Fear, I rebuke you, in Jesus Name!

- All fears must bow the knee to the name of Jesus, The Name of Jesus is above every name!

- When you use the name of Jesus in faith, you are making a demand just as if Jesus is making the demand!

** Importance of Communion in the Covenant**

- Every time you take communion, you should do so in remembrance of your covenant with God. We are to take communion often with this in mind.

1 Corinthians 11:23-26 - For I have received of the Lord that which also I delivered unto you, that the Lord Jesus the same night in which he was betrayed took bread:

24. And when he had given thanks, he broke it, and said, "Take, eat; this is my body, which is broken for you: this do in remembrance of me".

25. After the same manner also he took the cup, when he had supped, saying, "This cup is the new testament in my blood: this do ye, as oft as ye drink it, in remembrance of me".

26. For as often as ye eat this bread, and drink this cup, ye do show the Lord's death till he come.

- For as often as you eat this bread (representing Jesus' body broken for you) and drink this cup (representing Jesus' blood, shed for your sins) you do shew the Lord's death - you are acknowledging Jesus' sacrifice for you, that you are in covenant with God: Jesus, having paid the price for your total freedom: from spiritual death, sickness, disease, poverty, fear or anything that would steal, kill or destroy in your life.

Isaiah 53:4-5 - Surely he hath borne our griefs, and carried our sorrows: yet we did esteem him stricken, smitten of God, and afflicted,

5. But, he was wounded for our transgressions, he was bruised for our iniquities: The chastisement of our peace was upon him: and with his stripes, we are healed.

- This scripture - Isaiah 53:4-5 - tells us Jesus has provided everything that we need to be free from the curse. When we take communion we should be ready to receive forgiveness of our sins (when we judge ourselves and repent); salvation, peace of mind, healing, total prosperity, everything we need.

In Isaiah 53:4-5 - Jesus bore spiritual torment for our sins; mental distress for our worries, cares, and fear, and He bore physical pain for our sickness and disease. If He bore these things, we have a right to be free from them. We have a covenant with almighty God.

Galatians 3:29 - If ye be Christ's then are ye Abraham's seed, and heirs according to the promise.

- Receive your freedom from the curse of the law when you receive communion properly in faith.

To Receive Communion

Scripture: 1 Corinthians 11:23-24, Matthew 26:26-28, Luke 22:19-20

"Father God, in Jesus' name I (we) recognize that I (we) have a covenant with you - ratified by the shed blood of Jesus at Calvary. Jesus' body was broken for us, His blood was shed in our behalf, I (we) acknowledge that he bore sin, sickness, disease, sorrow, grief, fear, torment, unforgiveness, strife and lack for us. Through His substitutionary sacrifice we have complete redemption, total deliverance from the works of satan. As a new creature in Christ Jesus (I) we realize our freedom has been bought and paid for. We are (I am) forgiven, we are (I am) redeemed, and we (I) thank you for it all, in Jesus' name."

- Judge and EXAMINE YOURSELF ACCORDING TO God's word.

- Father, in Jesus' name, I (we) examine my (our) heart, and I (we) judge myself (ourselves) according to your word. "In all areas where I (we) have missed the mark (such as in strife, unforgiveness, jealousy, envy, hatred, covetousness, fear, worry, unbelief, or whatever). I (we) take Jesus as my (our) High Priest and Advocate. I (we) ask forgiveness according to the Word of God (1st John 1:9), your word says you are faithful and just to forgive us when we confess our sins and to cleanse us from all unrighteousness. I (we) receive my (our) forgiveness and cleansing in Jesus' Name. "Therefore I (we) do not eat of the bread, nor drink of the cup unworthily but I (we) rightly discern the Lord's body. I (we) receive communion now as the righteousness of God in Christ Jesus: (We are) I am free from the works of satan - spirit, soul, and body." I (we) judge any symptom of sickness in my (our) body (bodies) as being from satan, and I (we) refuse it, and receive the healing that Jesus has provided.

Confess: I (we) sanctify these elements as the Body and the Blood of Jesus in Jesus' Name. Amen.

Then Say:

"The Lord Jesus, the same night in which he was betrayed took bread: And when he had given thanks, he brake it, and said, Take, eat: this is my body, which is broken for you: this do in remembrance of me."

- Partake of The Bread

- Then Say this:

After the same manner also he took the cup, when he had supped, saying, This cup is the new Testament (covenant) in my blood: this do ye, as oft as ye drink it, in remembrance of me. For as often as ye eat this bread, and drink this cup, ye do shew the Lord's death till he come.

- Partake of The Cup

Make This Confession:

Father I (we) thank you for all you have provided for us (me) in Christ Jesus. I (we) confess this day, I (we) am the blessed of the Lord. This covenant we entered into at the new birth is a covenant filled with the exceeding great and precious promises of God and (we are) I am a partaker of those promises now!

I am (we are) healed. I am (we are) redeemed. I am (we are) delivered from the authority of darkness and translated into the kingdom of God's dear Son in whom I have redemption through His blood. I am (we are) the head and not the tail. I am (we are) above only and not beneath. I (we) come behind in no good thing. All that (we) I set my hands to prosper and I (we) praise you, Father, for the newness of life I (we) now enjoy, in Jesus' Name. Amen.

- Because you have a covenant with God:

- You have a Right to be Healed **

Isaiah 53:4-5 - Surely, He hath borne our griefs, and carried our sorrows.

- Surely is a covenant term. It means: Without a doubt, indisputable, unfailing, bound to come about, certain, a done deal!

Literally: Surely he has lifted, carried, or borne our sicknesses, diseases and our pains.

He was wounded for our transgressions, he was bruised for our iniquities, The chastisement of our peace with upon him, and with his stripes, we are healed.

- **1 Peter 2:24** - Who his own self bare our sins in His own body on the tree, that we, being dead to sin should live unto righteousness, by whose stripes, ye were healed.

- **Matthew 8:16-17** - When the even was come, they brought unto Him many that were possessed with devils, and He cast out the spirits with His word and healed all that were sick, that it might be fulfilled which was spoken by Esaias the Prophet saying, Himself took our infirmities, and bare our sicknesses.

NOTE: If Jesus took our infirmities, carried our diseases, bare our sins, we don't need to carry them or bare them. We have a right to stand against darkness and be free from sickness, disease, poverty, fear, failure or anything that the enemy brings against us to defeat us. We must fight the temptation to be defeated by applying the word of God, the Name of Jesus, and the power of the Holy Ghost! We have the assurance from God that all things are possible to anyone who believes. (Mark 9:23)

Making the Incurable: Curable (Or to Receive healing)

Applying the Principles

A. Connect with God

Connecting with God simply means being born-again or receiving Jesus as your Lord and Saviour.

1 Peter 1:23 - Being born again, not of corruptible seed, but of incorruptible, by the word of God, which liveth and abideth forever.

- How?

Romans 10:9-10 - That if thou shalt confess with thy mouth the Lord Jesus, and shalt believe in thine heart that God hath raised him from the dead, thou shalt be saved, For with the heart man believeth unto righteousness and with the mouth confession is made unto salvation.

Simply, Pray this Prayer: Father God in heaven, I come to you as a sinner, I repent of my sins, and I now ask you, Jesus, to be Lord and Saviour of my life. I believe in my heart that you died for my sins and that God raised you from the dead, so I now confess Jesus is my Lord. Thank you Father that I am born-again. Fill me with your Holy Spirit. I receive Him Now, in Jesus Name.

* (If you have prayed this prayer, contact us for Literature on the New Birth)*

Being born again is the most important decision (step) any human being can make. You are now connected to the Creator of the Universe in whom ALL THINGS ARE POSSIBLE. (Mark 10:27). Then be filled with His Spirit to have power in your life: Acts 1:8 - But ye shall receive power, after that the Holy Ghost is come upon you.

How?

Luke 11:9-10, 13 - And I say unto you, ask, and it shall be given you; seek, and ye shall find; knock, and it shall be opened unto you.

For everyone that asketh, receiveth; and he that seeketh, findeth; and to him that knocketh it shall be opened.

13. If ye then being evil (natural) know how to give good gifts unto your children: how much more shall your heavenly Father give the Holy Spirit to them that ask Him?

Ask:

Say: Father, In Jesus Name, your word says in Luke 11:13 - that you will give the `Holy Spirit to those who ask, so I am asking you now, fill me with your Holy Spirit, give me a language of prayer and praise. I receive in Jesus' Name, Thank you Lord.

- Note: once you are born-again, any one step or combinations can work for you to bring Healing.

- If you are seeking healing from God for any condition, especially an incurable one, you should seek His wisdom. James 1:5 – If any of you lack wisdom, let him ask of God, that giveth to all men liberally, and upbraideth not, and it shall be given him, and then pray in the Holy Ghost: Jude 20 - But ye beloved, building up yourselves on your most Holy faith, praying in the Holy Ghost. Keep yourselves in the Love of God.

Acts 2:4 - And they were all filled with the Holy Ghost, and began to speak with other tongues as the Spirit gave them utterance.

PRAY:

Father, in Jesus Name, I ask you for your wisdom concerning this condition, sickness – disease, etc. in my body. What do I need to do?

Once you have prayed, be listening for ideas, information, and insights. Stay in the Word, God speaks primarily through His Word.

He can also speak to you through an inward witness, through a vision or dream, directly to your spirit, or through others. But everything must be backed by what He has already said in His Word.

B. Walk in The Spirit

Decide to live by faith and walk in Love. You must have a forgiving heart: from your heart, forgive everyone who has wronged you, and seek forgiveness of anyone you have wronged.

Mark 11:25-26 - And when ye stand praying forgive, if ye have ought against any: that your Father also which is in heaven may forgive you your trespasses, But if ye do not forgive, neither will your Father forgive your trespasses. *Forgive, and Live!

(A study of the Law of the Spirit of Life under The Two Major Laws in chapter one will show you how to walk in the spirit).

CHAPTER THREE

The Power of the Word of God

Healing Scriptures

John 1:1 - In the beginning was the Word, and the Word was with God, and the Word was God.

- God's Word is the Cure!

Psalm 107:20 - He sent His word, and healed them, and delivered them from their destructions.

Proverbs 4:20-22 - My Son, attend to my Words; incline thine ear unto my sayings, Let them not depart from thine eyes; Keep them in the midst of thine heart, For they are life unto those that find them, and health to all their flesh. **Vs. 23** – keep thy heart with all diligence for out of it are the issues (forces) of life.

- God's word is life and health to all your flesh. *So keep your heart (spirit) full of God's word concerning healing and protect your heart (Mark 4:14-20).

- Read – MEDITATE – Listen To Healing Scriptures Continually.

- Listen to The New Testament on e-Bible, CD's, DVD's, MP3, I-Bible, etc.

- Listen to 'Anointed' Healing messages.

Just recently, I heard of a woman who was diagnosed as having multiple sclerosis. Upon hearing this, her husband, who is a minister of the Word and a firm believer in God's healing power, had her listening to healing words and messages 24 hours a day, 7 days a week. After a time of constantly, continually, hearing the 'healing word', she was completely healed!

3 John 1:2 - Beloved, I wish above all things that thou mayest prosper and be in health, even as thy soul prospereth.

1 John 5:14-15 - And this is the confidence that we have in Him, that if we ask anything according to His will, He heareth us: And if we know that he hear us, whatsoever we ask, we know that we have the petitions that we desired of him.

Isaiah 53: 4-5 - Surely he [Jesus] hath borne our griefs, and carried our sorrows (literal Hebrew: Surely He has lifted, carried or borne our sicknesses or diseases and our pains): yet we did esteem him stricken, smitten of God, and afflicted. But, He was wounded for our transgressions, he was bruised for our iniquities, the chastisement of our peace was upon him, and with his stripes we are healed.

Mark 16:17-18 - And these signs shall follow them that believe; In my name shall they cast out devils; they shall speak with new tongues; They shall take up serpents; and if they drink any deadly thing, it shall not hurt them; they shall lay hands on the sick and they shall recover.

(His Power is in His Word!)

Matthews 8:17 - That it might be fulfilled which was spoken by Isaiah the prophet, saying, Himself took our infirmities, and bare our sicknesses.

1-Peter 2:24 - Who his own self bare our sins in his own body on the tree, that we, being dead to sins, should live unto righteousness: by whose stripes ye were healed.

(WERE! WERE! WERE! – WERE is past tense!)

- Were means already – you are already healed!

Galatians 3:13-14, 29 - Christ hath redeemed us from the curse of the Law being made a curse for us: for it is written, cursed is everyone that hangeth on a tree: That the blessing of Abraham might come on the gentiles through Jesus Christ; that we might receive the promise of the spirit through faith –

29. And if ye be Christ's then are ye Abraham's seed, and heirs according to the promise.

Psalm 30:2 - O, Lord My God, I cried unto thee and thou hast healed me.

Psalm 34:19 - Many are the afflictions of the righteous; but the Lord delivereth him out of them all.

Psalm 42:11 - Hope thou in God: for I shall yet praise him, who is the health of my countenance, and my God.

Matthew 7:11 - If ye then being evil, (Natural) know how to give good gifts unto your children, how much more shall your Father which is in heaven give good things to them that ask him?

Colossians 1:12-14 - Giving thanks unto the Father, which hath made us meet (or able) to be partakers of the inheritance of the saints in light: Who hath delivered us from the power of darkness, and hath translated us into the kingdom of His dear Son: In whom we have redemption through his blood, even the forgiveness of sins.

Colossians 2:10, 15 - And ye are complete in Him, which is the head of all principality and power; and having spoiled principalities and powers, he made a shew of them openly, triumphing over them in it.

Hebrews 4:12-13 - For the Word of God is quick, and powerful, and sharper than any two-edged sword, piercing even to the dividing asunder of soul and spirit, and of the joints and marrow, and is a discerner of the thoughts and intents of the heart. Neither is there any creature that is not manifest in his sight: but all things are naked and opened unto the eyes of him with whom we have to do.

Hebrews 9:12 - Neither by the blood of goats and calves, but, by His own blood he entered in once into the holy place, having obtained eternal redemption for us.

Psalm 23:1 – The Lord is my shepherd, I shall not want.

Psalm 147:3 - He healeth the broken in heart, and bindeth up their wounds.

Psalm 103:3 - Who forgiveth all thine iniquities, who healeth all thy diseases;Who redeemeth thy life from destruction.

Psalm 105:37 - He brought them forth also with silver and gold; and there was not one feeble person among their tribes.

Psalm 67:2 - That thy way may be known upon earth, thy saving health among all nations.

Hebrews 1:3 - And upholding all things by the Word of His power ---

Job 37:23 - Touching the almighty, He is excellent in power and in judgment, and in plenty of justice: he will not afflict.

Psalm 145:8-9 - The Lord is gracious, and full of compassion, slow to anger and of great mercy. The Lord is good to all: and his tender mercies are over all His works.

2 Chronicles 16:9 - For the eyes of the Lord run to and fro throughout the whole earth, to show Himself strong in the behalf of them whose heart is perfect towards Him.

2 Chronicles 6:14 - O Lord God of Israel, there is no god like thee in the heaven, nor in the earth; which keepeth covenant, and shewest mercy unto thy servants, that walk before thee with all their hearts.

Numbers 23:19 - God is not a man, that he should lie; neither the son of man that he should repent: hath he said, and shall he not do it? Hath he spoken, and shall He not make it good?

2 Kings 20:5 - Turn again, and tell Hezekiah the captain of my people, Thus Saith the Lord, the God of David thy Father, I have heard thy prayer, I have seen thy tears; behold, I will heal thee.

2 Chronicles 30:20 - And the Lord hearkened to Hezekiah, and healed the people.

Genesis 20:17 - So Abraham prayed unto God: And God healed Abimelech, and his wife, and his maidservants; and they bare children.

Jeremiah 30:17 - For I will restore health unto thee, and I will heal thee of thy wounds, saith the Lord…

Jeremiah 33:6 - Behold, I will bring it health and cure, and I will cure them, and will reveal unto them the abundance of peace and truth.

Deuteronomy 30:19-20 - I call heaven and earth to record this day against you, that I have set before you life and death, blessing and cursing: therefore choose life that both thou and thy seed may live: That thou mayest love the Lord thy God, that thou mayest obey His voice, and that thou mayest cleave unto him: for he is thy life, and the length of thy days: that thou mayest dwell in the land which the Lord sware unto thy fathers…

Leviticus 26:3, 9 - If ye walk in my statutes, and keep my commandments, and do them…I will have respect unto you, and make you fruitful, and multiply you, and establish my covenant with you.

Isaiah 58: 8 - Then shall thy light break forth as the morning, and thine health shall spring forth speedily: and thy righteousness shall go before thee; the glory of the Lord shall be thy reward.

James 1:17 - Every good gift and every perfect gift is from above, and cometh down from the Father of Lights, with whom is no variableness, neither shadow of turning.

Romans 8:31 - If God be for us, who can be against us?

Malachi 3:6 - For I am the Lord, I change not!

Isaiah 41:10 - Fear thou not, for I am with thee; be not dismayed; for I am thy God: I will strengthen thee; yea, I will help thee; yea, I will uphold thee with the right hand of my righteousness.

Deuteronomy 7:15 - And the Lord will take away from thee all sickness, and will put none (permit none) of the evil diseases of Egypt, which thou knowest, upon thee.

Exodus 15:26 - If thou wilt diligently hearken to the voice of the Lord thy God, and wilt do that which is right in His sight, and wilt give ear to His commandments, and keep all his statutes, I will put none (PERMIT NONE) of these diseases upon thee, which I have permitted upon the Egyptians: For I am the Lord that healeth thee.

Hebrews 12:12-13 - Wherefore lift up the hands which hang down, and the feeble knees; and make straight paths for your feet, lest that which is lame be turned out of the way; but let it rather be healed.

Philippians 2:13 - For it is God who worketh in you, both to will and to do of His good pleasure.

Romans 8:32 - He that spared not his own Son, but delivered him up for us all, how shall he not with him also freely give us all things?

Ephesians 5:30 - For we are members of His body, of His flesh, and of His bones.

I Thessalonians 5:23 - And the very God of peace sanctify you wholly; and I pray God your whole spirit and soul and body be preserved blameless unto the coming of our Lord Jesus Christ.

Hosea 13:14 - I will ransom them from the power of the grave; I will redeem them from death: O death, I will be thy plagues; O grave, I will be thy destruction.

Exodus 20:12 - Honor thy father and thy mother: that thy days may be long upon the land which the Lord thy God giveth thee.

Deuteronomy 11:21 - That your days may be multiplied, and the days of your children, in the land which the Lord sware unto your fathers to give them, as the days of heaven upon the earth.

1 Chronicles 29:28 - And he (David) died in a good old age, full of days, riches and honour.

Job 5:26 - Thou shalt come to thy grave in a full age, like as a shock of corn cometh in his season.

Psalm 90:10 - The days of our years are three score years and ten; and if by reason of strength they be four score years ---

Proverbs 3:1-2 - My son, forget not my law, but let thine heart keep my commandments: for length of days, and long life, and peace, shall they add to thee.

Psalm 91:10 – 16 - There shall no evil befall thee, neither shall any plague come nigh thy dwelling.

11. For He shall give his angels charge over thee to keep thee in all thy ways,

12. They shall bear thee up in their hands, lest thou dash thy foot against a stone,

13. Thou shalt tread upon the lion and the adder: the young lion and the dragon shalt thou trample under feet

14. Because he hath set his love upon me, therefore will I deliver him: I will set him on high, because he hath known my name

15. He shall call upon me, and I will answer him: I will be with him in trouble; I will deliver him and honor him,

16. With long life will I satisfy him and show him my salvation.

Proverbs 9:11 - For by me thy days shall be multiplied, and the years of thy life shall be increased.

Ecclesiastes 7:17 - Why shouldest thou die before thy time?

Isaiah 40:31 - But they that wait upon the Lord shall renew their strength; they shall mount up with wings of eagles; they shall run and not be weary, they shall walk, and not faint.

Ephesians 6:1-3 - Children, obey your parents in the Lord: for this is right.

2.   Honor thy father and mother; which is the first commandment with Promise,

3.   That it may be well with thee, and thou mayest live long on the earth.

The Healing Ministry of Jesus

Matthew 8:14-17 - And when Jesus was come into Peter's house, he saw his wife's mother laid, and sick of a fever,

15.   And he touched her hand, and the fever left her: and she arose, and ministered unto them.

16.   When the even was come, they brought unto him many that were possessed with devils: and he cast out the spirits with his word, and healed all that were sick:

17.   That it might be fulfilled which was spoken by Esaias the prophet, saying, Himself took our infirmities, and bare our sicknesses.

Matthew 8:5-10, 13 - And when Jesus was entered into Capernaum, there came unto him a centurion, beseeching him,

6.   And saying, Lord, my servant lieth at home sick of the palsy, grievously tormented.

7.   And Jesus saith unto him, I will come and heal him,

8.   The centurion answered and said, Lord, I am not worthy that thou shouldest come under my roof: but speak the word only, and my servant shall be healed.

9.   For I am a man under authority; having soldiers under me: and I say to this man, go, and he goeth; and to another, come, and he cometh; and to my servant, Do this, and he doeth it.

10.   When Jesus heard it, he marveled, and said to them that followed, verily I say unto you, I have not found so great faith, no, not in Israel…

13.   And Jesus said unto the centurion, Go thy way; and as thou hast believed, so be it done unto thee, and his servant was healed in the same hour.

Matthew 8:2-3 - And behold, there came a leper and worshipped him, saying, Lord, if thou wilt, thou canst make me clean,

3. And Jesus put forth his hand, and touched him, saying, I will; be thou clean, and immediately his leprosy was cleansed.

Matthew 4:23-24 - And Jesus went about all Galilee, teaching in their synagogues, and preaching the gospel of the kingdom and healing all manner of sickness, and all manner of disease among the people.

NOTE: These scriptures tell us that there weren't just certain diseases that Jesus healed; all manner of sickness and all manner of disease refer to every kind of sickness and every kind of disease the people had: He healed them all! He is the same yesterday, and today, and forever. **Heb: 13:8**

Matthew 12:15 - But when Jesus knew it, he withdrew himself from thence: and great multitudes followed him, and he healed them all.

Matthew 9:20-22 - And behold, a woman, which was diseased with an issue of blood twelve years, came behind him, and touched the hem of his garment:

21. For she said within herself, if I may but touch his garment, I shall be whole.

22. But Jesus turned him about, and when He saw her, he said, Daughter, be of good comfort; thy faith hath made thee whole, and the woman was made whole from that hour.

Matthew 9:27-36 - And when Jesus was departed thence, two blind men followed him, crying and saying, Thou son of David, have mercy on us.

28. And when he was come into the house, the blind men came to Him: and Jesus saith unto them, believe ye that I am able to do this? They said unto him, yea Lord,

29. Then, touched he their eyes, saying, according to your faith be it unto you.

30. And their eyes were opened; and Jesus straightly charged them, saying, see that no man know it.

31. But they, when they were departed, spread abroad his fame in all that country.

32. As they went out; behold, they brought to him a dumb man possessed with a devil.

33. And when the devil was cast out, the dumb spoke: and the multitudes marveled, saying, it was never so seen in Israel.

34. But the Pharisees said, He castest out devils through the prince of the devils.

35. And Jesus went about all the cities and villages, teaching in their synagogues, and preaching the gospel of the kingdom, and healing every sickness and every disease among the people.

36. But when he saw the multitudes, he was moved with compassion on them, because they fainted, and were scattered abroad, as sheep having no shepherd.

Matthew 11:28-30 - Come unto me, all ye that labor, and are heavy laden, and I will give you rest,

29. Take my yoke upon you, and learn of me; for I am meek and lowly in heart: and ye shall find rest unto your souls.

30. For, my yoke is easy, and my burden is light.

Matthew 14:13-14 - When Jesus heard of it, he departed thence by ship into a desert place apart: and when the people had heard thereof, they followed him on foot out of the cities.

14. And Jesus went forth, and saw a great multitude, and was moved with compassion toward them, and he healed their sick.

Matthew 14:34-36 - And when they were gone over, they came into the land of Gennesaret,

35. And when the men of that place had knowledge of him, they sent out into all that country round about, and brought unto him all that were diseased;

36. And besought him that they might only touch the hem of his garment: and as many as touched were made perfectly whole.

Matthew 15:29-31 - And Jesus departed from thence, and came nigh unto the sea of Galilee; and went up into a mountain, and sat down there.

30. And great multitudes came unto him, having with them those that were lame, blind, dumb, maimed, and many others, and cast them down at Jesus' feet; and he healed them:

31. Insomuch that the multitude wondered, when they saw the dumb to speak, the maimed to be whole, the lame to walk, and the blind to see: and they glorified the God of Israel.

Mark 5:1-43 - And they came over unto the other side of the sea, into the country of the Gadarenes,

2. And when he was come out of the ship; immediately there met him out of the tombs a man with an unclean spirit;

3. Who had his dwelling among the tombs; and no man could bind him, no, not with chains,

4. Because that he had been often bound with fetters and chains, and the chains had been plucked asunder by him, and the fetters broken in pieces: neither could any man tame him,

5. And always, night and day, he was in the mountains, and in the tombs, crying, and cutting himself with stones.

6. And when he saw Jesus afar off, he ran and worshipped him,

7. And cried with a loud voice, and said, what have I to do with thee, Jesus, thou Son of the most high God? I adjure thee by God that thou torment me not.

8. For he said unto him, Come out of the man, thou unclean spirit.

9. And he asked him, what is thy name? And he answered my name is Legion: for we are many.

10. And he besought him much that he would not send them away out of the country.

11. Now there was there nigh unto the mountains a great herd of swine feeding,

12. And all the devils besought him, saying, send us into the swine that we may enter into them.

13. And forthwith Jesus gave them leave. And the unclean spirits went out, and entered into the swine: and the herd ran violently down a steep place into the sea, (they were about two thousand; and were choked in the sea.

14. And they that fed the swine fled, and told it in the city, and in the country. And they went out to see what it was that was done.

15. And they come to Jesus, and see him that was possessed with the devil, and had the Legion, sitting, and clothed, and in his right mind: and they were afraid.

16. And they that saw it told them how it befell to him that was possessed with the devil, and also concerning the swine,

17. And they began to pray him to depart out of their coast,

18. And when he was come into the ship, he that had been possessed with the devil prayed him that he might be with him,

19. Howbeit Jesus suffered him not, but saith unto him, Go home to thy friends, and tell them how great things the Lord hath done for thee, and hath had compassion on thee,

20. And he departed, and began to publish in Decapolis how great things Jesus had done for him: and all men did marvel.

21. And when Jesus was passed over again by ship unto the other side, much people gathered unto him: and he was nigh unto the sea.

22. And, behold, there cometh one of the rulers of the synagogue, Jairus by name; and when he saw him, he fell at his feet,

23. And besought him greatly, saying, My little daughter lieth at the point of death: I pray thee, come and lay thy hands on her, that she may be healed, and she shall live.

24. And Jesus went with him; and much people followed him, and thronged him.

25. And a certain woman, which had an issue of blood twelve years,

26. And had suffered many things of many physicians, and had spent all that she had, and was nothing bettered, but rather grew worse,

27.   When she had heard of Jesus, came in the press behind, and touched his garment.

28.   For she said, If I may but touch his clothes, I shall be whole.

29.   And straightway the fountain of her blood was dried up; and she felt in her body that she was healed of that plague.

30.   And Jesus, immediately knowing in himself that virtue had gone out of him, turned him about in the press, and said, Who touched my clothes?

31.   And his disciples said unto him, Thou seest the multitude thronging thee, and sayest thou, who touched me?

32.   And he looked round about to see her that had done this thing.

33.   But the woman fearing and trembling, knowing what was done to her, came and fell down before him, and told him all the truth.

34.   And he said unto her, Daughter, thy faith hath made thee whole; go in peace, and be whole of thy plague.

35.   And while He yet spake, there came from the ruler of the synagogue's house certain which said, Thy daughter is dead: Why troublest thou the Master any further?

36.   As soon as Jesus heard the word that was spoken, he saith unto the ruler of the synagogue, Be not afraid, only believe.

37.   And he suffered no man to follow him, save Peter, and James, and John the brother of James.

38.   And he cometh to the house of the ruler of the synagogue, and seeth the tumult, and them that wept and wailed greatly.

39.   And when he was come in, he saith unto them, Why make ye this ado, and weep? the damsel is not dead, but sleepeth.

40.   And they laughed him to scorn. But when he had put them all out, he taketh the father and mother of the damsel, and them that were with him, and entered in where the damsel was lying.

41.   And he took the damsel by the hand, and said unto her, Talitha cumi; which is, being interpreted, Damsel, I say unto thee, arise.

42.   And straightway the damsel arose, and walked; for she was of the age of twelve years. And they were astonished with a great astonishment.

43.   And he charged them straitly that no man should know it; and commanded that something should be given her to eat.

Mark 6:53-56 - And when they had passed over, they came into the Land of Gennesaret, and drew to the shore.

54. And when they were come out of the ship, straightway they knew him,

55. And ran through that whole region round about, and began to carry about in beds those that were sick where they heard he was,

56. And whithersoever he entered, into villages, or cities, or country, they laid the sick in the streets, and besought him that they might touch if it were but the border of his garment: and as many as touched him were made whole.

Mark 7:25-37 - For a certain woman, whose young daughter had an unclean spirit, heard of him and came and fell at his feet:

26. The woman was a Greek, a Syrophenician by nation; and she besought him that he would cast forth the devil out of her daughter.

27. But Jesus said unto her, Let the children first be filled: for it is not meet to take the children's bread, and to cast it unto the dogs.

28. And she answered and said unto him, Yes, Lord: yet the dogs under the table eat of the children's crumbs.

29. And he said unto her, For this saying go thy way; the devil is gone out of thy daughter.

30. And when she was come to her house, she found the devil gone out, and her daughter laid upon the bed.

31. And again, departing from the coast of Tyre and Sidon, he came unto the sea of Galilee, through the midst of the coast of Decapolis.

32. And they bring unto him one that was deaf, and had an impediment in his speech; and they beseech him to put his hand upon him.

33. And he took him aside from the multitude and put his fingers into his ears, and he spit, and touched his tongue;

34. And looking up to heaven, he sighed, and saith unto him, Ephphatha: that is, Be opened.

35. And straightway his ears were opened, and the string of his tongue was loosed, and he spake plain.

36. And he charged them that they should tell no man: but the more he charged them, so much the more a great deal they published it;

37. And were beyond measure astonished, saying, He hath done all things well: he maketh both the deaf to hear, and the dumb to speak.

Mark 9:17-29 – And one of the multitude answered and said, Master, I have brought unto thee my son, which hath a dumb spirit;

18. And wherever he taketh him, he teareth him: and he foameth, and gnashed with his teeth, and pineth away: and I spake to thy disciples that they should cast him out; and they could not.

19. He answereth him, and saith, O faithless generation, how long shall I be with you? how long shall I suffer you? Bring him unto me.

20. And they brought him unto him: and when he saw him, straightway the spirit tare him; and he fell on the ground, and wallowed foaming.

21. And he asked his father, How long is it ago since this came unto him? And he said, of a child.

22. And ofttimes it hath cast him into the fire, and into the waters, to destroy him: but if thou canst do anything; have compassion on us, and help us.

23. Jesus said unto him, If thou canst believe, all things are possible to him that believeth.

    NOTE: ALL THINGS!

24. And straightway the father of the child cried out and said with tears, Lord, I believe; help thou mine unbelief.

25. When Jesus saw that the people came running together, he rebuked the foul spirit, saying unto him, Thou dumb and deaf spirit, I charge thee, come out of him, and enter no more into him.

26. And the spirit cried, and rent him sore, and came out of him: and he was as one dead; insomuch that many said, He is dead.

27. But Jesus took him by the hand, and lifted him up; and he arose.

28. And when he was come into the house, his disciples asked him privately, Why could not we cast him out?

29. And he said unto them, This kind can come forth by nothing, but by prayer and fasting.

Luke 4:16-21 – And he came to Nazareth, where he had been brought up: and, as his custom was, he went into the synagogue on the Sabbath day, and stood up for to read.

17. And there was delivered unto him the book of the prophet Esaias. And when he had opened the book, he found the place where it was written,

18. The Spirit of the Lord is upon me, because he hath anointed me to preach the gospel to the poor; he hath sent me to heal the broken- hearted, to preach deliverance to the captives, and recovering of sight to the blind, to set at liberty them that are bruised,

19. To preach the acceptable year of the Lord.

20. And he closed the book, and he gave it again to the minister, and sat down. And the eyes of all them that were in the synagogue were fastened on him.

21. And he began to say unto them, This day is this scripture fulfilled in your ears.

Luke 4:33-36, 40-41 – And in the synagogue there was a man, which had an unclean devil, and cried out with a loud voice,

34. Saying, Let us alone; what have we to do with thee, thou Jesus of Nazareth? Art thou come to destroy us? I know thee who thou art; the Holy One of God.

35. And Jesus rebuked him, saying, Hold thy peace, and come out of him. And when the devil had thrown him in the midst, he came out of him, and hurt him not.

36. And they were all amazed, and spake among themselves, saying, What a word is this! For with authority and power he commandeth the unclean spirits, and they come out.

40. Now when the sun was setting, all they that had any sick with divers diseases brought them unto him; and he laid his hands on every one of them, and healed them.

41. And devils also came out of many, crying out, and saying, Thou art Christ the Son of God. And he, rebuking them suffered them not to speak: for they knew that he was Christ.

John 10:10 – The thief cometh not, but for to steal, and to kill, and to destroy: I am come that they might have life, and that they might have it more abundantly.

Luke 6:6-10 – And it came to pass also on another Sabbath, that he entered into the synagogue and taught: and there was a man whose right hand was withered.

7. And the scribes and Pharisees watched him, whether he would heal on the Sabbath day; that they might find an accusation against him.

8. But he knew their thoughts, and said to the man which had the withered hand, Rise up, and stand forth in the midst. And he arose and stood forth.

9. Then said Jesus unto them, I will ask you one thing; Is it lawful on the Sabbath days to do good, or to do evil? To save life, or to destroy it?

10. And looking round about upon them all, he said unto the man, Stretch forth thy hand. And he did so: and his hand was restored whole as the other.

Luke 6:17-19 – And he came down with them, and stood in the plain, and the company of his disciples, and a great multitude of people out of all Judea and Jerusalem, and from the sea coast of Tyre and Sidon, which came to hear him, and to be healed of their diseases.

18. And they that were vexed with unclean spirits: and they were healed.

19. And the whole multitude sought to touch him: for there went virtue out of him, and healed them all.

Luke 13:11-17 - And, behold, there was a woman which had a spirit of infirmity eighteen years, and was bowed together, and could in no wise lift up herself.

12. And when Jesus saw her, he called her to him, and said unto her, Woman, thou art loosed from thine infirmity.

13. And he laid his hands on her: and immediately she was made straight, and glorified God.

14. And the ruler of the synagogue answered with indignation, because that Jesus had healed on the Sabbath day, and said unto the people, There are six days in which men ought to work: in them therefore come and be healed, and not on the Sabbath day.

15. The Lord then answered him, and said, Thou hypocrite, doth not each one of you on the sabbath loose his ox or his ass from the stall, and lead him away to watering?

16. And ought not this woman, being a daughter of Abraham, whom Satan hath bound, lo, these eighteen years, be loosed from this bond on the Sabbath day?

17. And when he had said these things, all his adversaries were ashamed: and all the people rejoiced for all the glorious things that were done by him.

John 5:2-14 - Now there is at Jerusalem by the sheep market a pool, which is called in the Hebrew tongue Bethesda, having five porches.

3. In these lay a great multitude of impotent folk, of blind, halt, withered, waiting for the moving of the water.

4. For an angel went down at a certain season into the pool, and troubled the water: whosoever then first after the troubling of the water stepped in was made whole of whatsoever disease he had.

5. And a certain man was there, which had an infirmity thirty and eight years.

6. When Jesus saw him lie, and knew that he had been now a long time in that case, he saith unto him, wilt thou be made whole?

7. The impotent man answered him, Sir, I have no man, when the water is troubled, to put me into the pool: but while I am coming, another steppeth down before me.

8. Jesus saith unto him, Rise, take up thy bed and walk.

9. And immediately the man was made whole, and took up his bed, and walked: and on the same day was the Sabbath.

10. The Jews therefore said unto him that was cured, It is the Sabbath day: it is not lawful for thee to carry thy bed.

11. He answered them, He that made me whole, the same said unto me, Take up thy bed, and walk.

12. Then asked they him, What man is that which said unto thee, Take up thy bed, and walk?

13. And he that was healed wist not who it was: for Jesus had conveyed himself away, a multitude being in that place.

14. Afterward Jesus findeth him in the temple, and said unto him, Behold, thou art made whole: sin no more, lest a worse thing come upon thee.

John 9:1-7 - And as Jesus passed by, he saw a man which was blind from his birth.

2. And his disciples asked him, saying, Master, who did sin, this man, or his parents, that he was born blind?

3. Jesus answered, Neither hath this man sinned, nor his parents: but that the works of God should be made manifest in him.

4. I must work the works of him that sent me, while it is day: the night cometh, when no man can work.

5. As long as I am in the world, I am the light of the world.

6. When he had thus spoken, he spat on the ground, and made clay of the spittle, and he anointed the eyes of the blind man with the clay,

7. And said unto him, Go, wash in the pool of Siloam, (which is by interpretation, Sent.) He went his way therefore, and washed, and came seeing.

Acts 10:38 - How God anointed Jesus of Nazareth with the Holy Ghost, and with power, who went about doing good and healing all that were oppressed of the devil; for God was with him.

Hebrews 13:8 - Jesus Christ, the same yesterday and today, and forever.

John 3:8 - He that committeth sin is of the devil; for the devil sinneth from the beginning. For this purpose the Son of God was manifested, that he might destroy the works of the devil.

Matthew 10:1 - And when he had called unto him his twelve disciples, he gave them power against unclean spirits, to cast them out, and to heal all manner of sickness and all manner of disease.

Mark 16:15-20 - And he said unto them, Go ye into all the world, and preach the gospel to every creature.

16. He that believeth and is baptized shall be saved; but he that believeth not shall be damned.

17. And these signs shall follow them that believe; In my name shall they cast out devils; they shall speak with new tongues;

18. They shall take up serpents; and if they drink any deadly thing, it shall not hurt them; they shall lay hands on the sick, and they shall recover.

19. So then after the Lord had spoken unto them, he was received up into heaven, and sat on the right hand of God.

20. And they went forth and preached every where, the Lord working with them, and confirming the word with signs following. Amen

John 14:12-15 - Verily, verily, I say unto you, He that believeth on me, the works that I do shall he do also; and greater works than these shall he do; because I go unto my Father.

13. And whatsoever ye shall ask in my name, that will I do, that the Father may be glorified in the Son.

14. If ye shall ask any thing in my name, I will do it.

15. If ye love me, keep my commandments.

Acts 8:6-7 - And the people with one accord gave heed unto those things which Phillip spake, hearing and seeing the miracles which he did.

7. For unclean spirits, crying out with loud voice, came out of many that were possessed with them: and many taken with palsies, and that were lame, were healed.

Acts 9:33-34 - And there he found a certain man named Aeneas, which had kept his bed eight years, and was sick of the palsy.

34. And Peter said unto him, Aeneas, Jesus Christ maketh thee whole: arise, and make thy bed. And he arose immediately.

Acts 14:8-10 – And there sat a certain man at Lystra, impotent in his feet, being a cripple from his mother's womb, who never had walked:

9. The same heard Paul speak: Who steadfastly beholding him, and perceiving that he had faith to be healed,

10. Said with a loud voice, Stand upright on thy feet. And he leaped and walked.

Acts 19:11-12 – And God wrought special miracles by the hands of Paul:

12. So that from his body were brought unto the sick handkerchiefs or aprons, and the diseases departed from them, and the evil spirits went out of them.

Malachi 4:2 - But unto you that fear my name shall the Sun of Righteousness arise with healing in his wings; and ye shall go forth and grow up as calves of the stall.

James 5:14-16 - Is any sick among you? Let him call for the elders of the church; and let them pray over him, anointing him with oil in the name of the Lord:

15. And the prayer of faith shall save the sick, and the Lord shall raise him up; and if he have committed sins, they shall be forgiven him.

16. Confess your faults one to another, and pray one for another, that ye may be healed. The effectual fervent prayer of a righteous man availeth much.

Hebrews 1:1-4 - God, who at sundry times and in divers manners spoke in time past unto the fathers by the prophets,

2. Hath in these last days spoken unto us by his Son, whom he hath appointed heir of all things, by whom also he made the worlds;

3. Who being the brightness of his glory, and the express image of his person, and upholding all things by the word of his power, when he had by himself purged our sins, sat down on the right hand of the Majesty on high;

4. Being made so much better than the angels, as he hath by inheritance obtained a more excellent name than they.

Philippians 2:8-11 - And being found in fashion as a man, he humbled himself, and became obedient unto death, even the death of the cross.

9. Wherefore God also hath highly exalted him, and given him a name which is above every name:

10. That at the name of Jesus every knee should bow, of things (beings) in heaven, and things (beings) in earth, and things (beings) under the earth;

11. And that every tongue should confess that Jesus Christ is Lord, to the glory of God the Father.

Matthew 18:19 – Again I say unto you, That if two of you shall agree on earth as touching anything that they shall ask, it shall be done for them of my Father which is in heaven.

Mark 11:22-26 – And Jesus answering saith unto them, Have faith in God.

23. For verily I say unto you, That whosoever shall say unto this mountain, Be thou removed, and be thou cast into the sea; and shall not doubt in his heart, but shall believe that those things which he saith shall come to pass; he shall have whatsoever he saith.

24. Therefore I say unto you, What things soever ye desire when ye pray, believe that ye receive them, and ye shall have them.

25. And when ye stand praying, forgive, if you have ought against any: that your Father also which is in heaven may forgive your trespasses.

26.   But if ye do not forgive, neither will your Father which is in heaven forgive your trespasses.

Romans 4:17, 19-21 – (As it is written, I have made thee a father of many nations) before him whom he believed, even God, who quickeneth the dead, and called those things which be not as though they were…

19.   And being not weak in Faith, He considered not his own body, now dead when he was about an hundred years old, neither yet the deadness of Sarah's womb:

20.   He staggered not at the promise of God through unbelief, but was strong in faith, giving glory of God;

21.   And being fully persuaded that, what he had promised, he was able also to perform.

Romans 10:17 - So then faith cometh by hearing, and hearing by the word of God.

1 Timothy 6:12 - Fight the good fight of faith, lay hold on eternal life, whereunto thou art also called, and hast professed a good profession before many witnesses.

Hebrews 11:1 - Now faith is the substance of things hoped for, the evidence of things not seen.

Hebrews 11:6 - But without faith it is impossible to please him: for he that cometh to God must believe that he is, and that he is a rewarder of them that diligently seek him.

1 John 5:4-5 - For whatsoever is born of God overcometh the world: and this is the victory that overcomes the world, even our faith.

5.   Who is he that overcometh the world, but he that believeth that Jesus is the Son of God?

God Wants You Well

1 Corinthians 3:16 - Know ye not, that ye are the temple of God, and that the Spirit of God dwells in you?

Romans 8:2 - For the Law of the Spirit of Life in Christ Jesus, hath made me free from the Law of sin and death.

1 John 4:4 - Ye are of God, little children, and have over come them: because greater is he that is in you, than he that is in the world.

Romans 8:11 - But if the Spirit of him that raised up Jesus from the dead dwell in you, he that raised up Christ from the dead shall also Quicken (make alive) your mortal bodies by his Spirit that dwelleth in you.

Philippians 2:13 - For it is God which worketh in you, both to will and to do of his good pleasure.

James 4:7-8 - Submit yourselves therefore to God. Resist the devil, and he will flee from you. Draw nigh to God, and He will draw nigh to you.

2 Timothy 1:7 - For God hath not given us the spirit of fear; but of power, and of love, and of a sound mind.

Hebrews 2:14-15 - Forasmuch then as the children are partakers of flesh and blood he also himself likewise took part of the same, that through death he might destroy him who had the power of death, that is, the devil;

15.   And deliver them who through fear of death were all their lifetime subject to bondage.

Romans 6:14 - For sin shall not have dominion over you: for ye are not under the Law, but under grace.

Psalm 107:20 - He sent his word, and healed them, and delivered them from their destructions.

John 15:7 - If ye abide in me, and my words abide in you, ye shall ask what ye will, and it shall be done unto you.

Matthew 4:14 - But he answered and said, It is written, man shall not live by bread alone, but by every word that proceeded out of the mouth of God.

Matthew 8:16 - When the even was come, they brought unto him many that were possessed with devils: and he cast out the spirits with his word, and healed all that were sick.

John 1:1,14 - In the beginning was the word, and the word was with God and the word was God…

14.   And the word was made flesh, and dwelth among us (and we beheld his glory as of the only begotten of the Father) full of grace and truth.

Isaiah 55:11 - So shall my word be that goeth forth out of my mouth: it shall not return unto me void, but it shall accomplish that which I please, and it shall prosper in the thing where to I sent it.

Psalm 118:17 - I shall not die, but live and declare the works of the Lord.

Isaiah 40:29 - He giveth power to the faint; and to them that have no might, he increaseth strength.

Isaiah 41:10 - Fear thou not: for I am with thee, be not dismayed, for I am thy God: I will strengthen thee; yea, I will help thee; yea, I will uphold thee with the right hand of my righteousness.

Nahum 1:9 - What do ye imagine against the Lord? He will make an utter end: affliction shall not rise up the second time.

2 Corinthians 4:18 - While we look not at the things which are seen, but at the things which are not seen; for the things which are seen are temporal; but the things which are not seen are eternal.

Ephesians 6:10-18 - Finally, by brethren, be strong in the Lord, and in the power of his might.

11. Put on the whole armor of God, that ye may be able to stand against the wiles of the devil.

12. For we wrestle not against flesh and blood, but against principalities, against powers, against the rulers of the darkness of this world, against spiritual wickedness in high places.

13. Wherefore take unto you the whole armor of God, that ye may be able to withstand in the evil day, and having done all, to stand.

14. Stand therefore, having your loins girt about with truth, and having on the breastplate of righteousness;

15. And your feet shod with the preparation of the gospel of peace;

16. Above all, taking the shield of faith, wherewith ye shall be able to quench all the fiery darts of the wicked.

17. And take the helmet of salvation, and the sword of the Spirit, which is the word of God:

18. Praying always with all prayer and supplication in the Spirit, and watching thereunto with all perseverance and supplication for all saints.

Mark 10:27 - And Jesus looking upon them saith, with men it is impossible, but not with God: for with God all things are possible.

2 Timothy 1:7 - For God hath not given us the spirit of fear, but of power, and of love, and of a sound mind.

Hebrews 10:35-36 - Cast not away therefore your confidence, which hath great recompense of reward.

36. For ye have need of patience, that, after ye have done the will of God, ye might receive the promise.

Hebrews 11:11 - Through faith also Sara herself received strength to conceive seed, and was delivered of a child when she was past age, because she judged him faithful who had promised.

1 John 3:21-23 - Beloved, if our heart condemn us not, then have we confidence toward God.

22. And whatsoever we ask, we receive of him, because we keep His commandments and do those things that are pleasing in His sight.

23. And this is his commandment, that we should believe on the name of his Son Jesus Christ, and love one another, as he gave us commandment.

Matt 18:18-20

Verily I say unto you, whatsoever ye shall bind on earth shall be bound in heaven: and whatsoever ye shall loose on earth shall be loosed in heaven.

19. Again I say unto you, that if two of you shall agree on earth as touching anything that they shall ask, it shall be done for them of my Father which is in heaven.

20. For where two or three are gathered together in my name, there am I in the midst of them.

CHAPTER FOUR

The Power of Prayer

Mark 11:24 - Therefore, I say unto you, what things soever you desire, when ye pray, believe that ye receive them and ye shall have them.

- There is tremendous power in prayer!

James 5:16 - Confess your faults one to another, and pray one for another, that ye may be healed. The effectual fervent prayer of a righteous man availeth much.

The Amplified Bible says, The earnest (heartfelt), (continued) prayer of a righteous man makes tremendous power available (dynamic in it's working.) So we shouldn't take our prayers lightly. We should pray expecting God to hear and answer.

Isaiah 30:19 - He will be very gracious unto thee at the voice of thy cry; when he shall hear it, he will answer thee.

1 John 5:14-15 - and this is the confidence that we have in him, that if we ask anything according to his will, he hears us:

15.   And if we know that he hear us, whatsoever we ask, we know that we have the petitions that we desired of Him.

- Ask for anything (in faith) according to his will, (His word is His will) we know that we have the answer.

- **Now Lets Define Prayer:**

Prayer is to "voice a desire" – an asking; entreaty; supplication or request; a petition to a superior; communication or fellowship. There are several kinds of prayer, but to be effective we must pray to God the Father, the Creator (and not to some "universal being" or other gods or beings,) and we are to pray in Jesus' Name, since He, through his substitutionary sacrifice on the cross made it possible for us to be reconnected to God, and to be healed divinely or supernaturally.

We know that prayer changes things, so we are not out to change God, because He never changes (Malachi 3:6 - For I am the Lord, I change not.)

So we are to know what God's word says about a situation, and allow the word to change the situation, for instance if you are faced with a symptom of sickness or disease, the Word of God in 1 Peter 2:24 says "By whose stripes ye were healed. Your faith in the word "By whose stripes ye were healed" and your prayer, confession and continual standing on that word will cause your body to get in line with God's word. In other words, if you believe the word of God, and 'see' the word as being more real than the symptoms in your body, your body will become as the word implies, "Ye were healed".

Seven Steps to Answered Prayer

#1. Be specific

Know what you want God to do for you, then search the scriptures and see what the word of God says about your particular need. For example, if you need wisdom concerning how to deal with a certain thing, James 1:5 says, "If any of you lack wisdom, let him ask of God," or in the case of healing: Isaiah 53:4-5; Matthew 8:17; 1 Peter 2:24 are scriptures you can stand and rely on, and then pray according to the word. Meditate (Play a Picture in your mind as seeing yourself healed and in good health!)

(Also read and re-read the section on meditation)

The word is your sword against the devil and all the demons of hell that would come against your body to cause ill health.

Continually meditate or think about what the word says and voice it aloud when contrary thoughts come to your mind.

#2. Pray to God the Father in Jesus' Name

John 16:23-24 - And in that day ye shall ask me nothing, verily, verily I say unto you, whatsoever ye shall ask the Father in my name, he will give it you.

24. Hitherto have ye asked nothing in my name: ask, and ye shall receive, that your joy may be full.

Once you have asked God for what you need: Believe you receive* (When you pray), Mark 11:24 - Therefore I say unto you, what things soever ye desire, *when ye pray, believe that ye receive them and ye shall have them. When you pray, believe that you receive, not after you feel better. You may feel better after you pray or you may not. That is no indication that God has not heard and answered your prayer. *Sometimes healing comes by degrees; If you don't feel better immediately, or, even if you feel worse, don't be moved by your feelings! Believe that the moment you pray, God has heard and answered because you prayed according to the word of God and you have asked in faith.

Matthew 21:22 - And all things, whatever ye shall ask in prayer, believing, ye shall receive.

- You have to believe you have it before you get it!

*You must realize that the devil, your enemy, operates in the sensual, feeling realm. He tries to get you to go by what you see or feel instead of what you believe. This is why you need to look to God's word and believe what the word says over all other contrary circumstances. God's word is supernatural and it produces a supernatural cure!

#3. Stay Positive

Keep your mind on the word and cast down every thought that suggest you don't have the answer.

2 Corinthians 10:5 - Casting down imaginations, and every high thing that exalts itself against the knowledge of God, and bringing into captivity every thought to the obedience of Christ. – Any reasoning or mental picture that comes to your mind that doesn't agree with the Word of God, cast it down!

1 Peter 2:24 - Who His own self bare our sins in His own body on the tree, that we, being dead to sins, should live unto righteousness, by whose stripes ye were healed.

- Refuse: doubt, fear and unbelief, they are of the devil.

James 4:7 - Submit yourselves therefore to God. Resist the devil, and he will flee from you.

You submit to God by submitting to His Word. Hold on to what the word says regardless of feelings, circumstances and everything that contradicts the word of God.

- Think only and talk only what you believe. Believe God has heard and answered, and Stand!

(Also Read Section on Confessions and Meditation)

- Actively pursue your answer – you will never obtain what you are not willing to pursue.
- To stay positive you must also think positive, act positive and speak positive.

Proverbs 23:7 - For as he thinketh in his heart, so is he.

#4. Guard Your Mind

Your mind acts as a gateway to your spirit, (or heart)

Proverbs 4:23 - Keep thy heart with all diligence; for out of it are the issues of life.

Keep your heart with all diligence. Watch what goes into your heart! How do things get into your heart? Thoughts, ideas, suggestions, doubts, etc, come to your mind. If you receive them, you will begin to speak them. When you speak, or say a thing repeatedly, or over and over, your spirit picks up these thoughts, ideas, etc, and acts on them to bring them to pass in your life. (Remember the Parable of the Sower) Mark 4:14-20.

- Again, you cast down imaginations, and every high thing that exalts itself against the knowledge (or the word) of God, and make every thought obey the word. Refuse every thought that your prayer is not answered.

You may have to disassociate yourself from Negative talking, cynical people, even religious people who don't believe in divine healing, (They will destroy your faith!) Stay away from churches that don't believe in divine healing and find one that believe in faith, and healing, and living the word of God.

#5. Meditate on God's Promises

Meditate - imagine yourself with the answer. Do this constantly, consistently. The word of God in Isaiah 53:5 – He was wounded for our transgressions, He was bruised for our iniquities, the chastisement of our peace was upon Him, and with His stripes we are healed. Are healed, NOW!

For you to be healed, 'see' yourself as healed – Now! (regardless of how you feel, look, or otherwise). Don't let the word depart from your eyes. See yourself as the word sees you: "we arc healed" (present tense).

Proverbs 4:20-22 - My son attend to my words; incline thine ear unto my sayings (and keep listening)

21. Let them not depart from thine eyes; Keep them in the midst of thine heart,

22. For they (my words) are life unto those that find them and health (medicine) unto all their flesh.

- God's word is medicine to all your flesh. They are Life to those that find them and health (medicine, healing) to all your flesh.

(Read, Meditate the section on MEDITATION)

#6. Praise and Thank God Continually

- Praise to God is vitally important. It helps you to be aware that God is present and that He does care about your well being. Praise also stops the enemy attacks against you. God has ordained praise to stop the enemy – Psalm 8:2 – Out of the mouth of babes and sucklings hast thou ordained strength (Praise) because of thine enemies, that thou mightest still (stop) the enemy and the avenger.

If you believe you have what you asked God for, then praise and thank God for the answer, even if you don't see or feel a manifestation, praise and thanksgiving will boost your faith and speed up the results you desire. Remember God wants to answer your prayers, but there are spiritual laws we must abide by. God is bound also by His own laws, Faith is a Law – Romans 3:27 – Where is boasting then? It is excluded. By what law? of works? Nay: but by the Law of faith.

- Part of the Law of faith is acting as it is already done. When you act as if it is already done, then faith goes to work to bring it to pass, and praise and thanksgiving shows that you are expecting!

Mark 11:23 - For verily I say unto you, That whosoever shall say unto this mountain, be thou removed, and be thou cast into the sea; and shall not doubt in his heart, but shall believe that those things which he saith shall come to pass, He shall have whatsoever he saith. (says)

"Whosoever shall say unto this mountain, He shall have whatsoever he saith." You might see or feel as though a sickness, disease or condition in your body as a 'mountain' in your life, 'praise' and 'thanksgiving' are 'sayings': Imagine every time you thank God or praise Him, that mountain is being chipped down to size.

Every time you praise, every time you praise, Every time you give thanks, every time, that 'mountain' is being leveled down to the ground, eventually you will have whatsoever you say! (He shall have whatsoever he saith.)

(Also Refer to the section on Thanksgiving, Praise And Worship)

#7. Speak Only Faith

Once you have prayed about a particular thing in faith, you don't need to continually pray the same prayer, asking for the same thing over and over. Once you have prayed the prayer of faith about a particular situation, stand your ground. Refuse to talk anything contrary to what you have prayed about. Think and speak only faith thoughts and words. Unbelief will stop the answer!

- We stated that prayer is our connection with God. It was said by John Wesley (The founder of the Methodist Church) that: "It seems God is limited by our prayer life: That He can do nothing for humanity unless someone asks him".

- We need to know also that there are different kinds of prayer, and there are different rules that apply to them. Ephesians 6:18 , Praying always with all prayer and supplication in the spirit, and watching thereunto with all perseverance and supplication for the saints.

"Praying with all kinds of Prayer" one translation reads. Just as you don't use the same rules of football to play basketball so there are different rules in prayer.

*Let's look at the different Kinds of Prayer.

1. Prayer of Dedication and Consecration

Matthew 26:36-39 - Then cometh Jesus with them unto a place called Gethsemane, and saith unto his disciples, Sit ye here, while I go and pray yonder.

37. And he took with him Peter and the two sons of Zebedee, and began to be sorrowful and very heavy.

38. Then he saith unto them, My soul is exceeding sorrowful, even unto death: tarry ye here, and watch with me.

39. And he went a little farther, and fell on his face, and prayed, saying, O my Father, if it be possible, let this cup pass from me: nevertheless not as I will, but as thou wilt.

- The phrase "If it be thy will" has crippled the faith of many who are seeking healing. God's word is his will!" By whose stripes ye were healed, 1 Peter 2:24 and "I am the Lord that healeth thee "Exodus 15:26, are just two of the many scriptures that tell us clearly what God's will is concerning healing and health, and we are never to use the phrase: "If it be thy will when we are praying for healing or anything where the word of God states God's will about the matter, for instance 3-John 2, Beloved I wish (I will) above all things that thou mayest prosper and be in health, even as thy soul prospers. It is God's will that you prosper – and, be in health!

2. The Prayer of Commitment

1 Peter 5:6-7 - Humble yourselves therefore under the mighty hand of God, that He may exalt you in due time, casting all your cares on Him; for He careth for you.

Philippians 4:6-7 - Be careful for nothing; but in everything by prayer and supplication with thanksgiving let your request be known unto God, and the peace of God, which passeth all understanding shall keep your hearts and minds through Christ Jesus.

Don't fret or be anxious about anything. We must cast (like throwing away) every worried thought over on God. If God says not to worry or be anxious for anything, then that is exactly what He means!

- Cast your cares on God and don't take them back!

Example: Father, in Jesus' name, we commit this (situation) to you, and we roll all the cares of it over on you. Thank you.

When the thought comes back to your mind to cause you to worry or fear, you must reject them by saying "I rolled all my cares on God, I refuse to worry or fear", and then form in your mind the answer of being completely free of that situation.

- I remember something that happened over 30 years ago that still has an effect on me concerning getting rid of worry. My tour of duty in the Army was about to end, so I was sent to the Med Center for a pre-release physical. When they checked my blood pressure, they found that it was higher than normal. During the review of the physical the physician asked me the question: "What are you worrying about?" (in reference to the high blood pressure reading), it kind of shocked me because I had never related worry to high blood pressure, but one thing I did after that was to be aware of every occasion I had to worry and, by my will, chose not to worry. When I went back to the clinic (about two weeks later), my blood pressure was normal! (And I didn't know God at that time). Now, since I have been born again, for the past 40 plus years, I have not had any headaches, and I often teach, that I used to be a "worry addict," taking nerve medications, aspirins and headache powders, which were of little help – and sometimes made conditions worse, especially, the nerve medications.

I went to the Emergency Room once because of a 'bad case' of depression, and was given a prescription for an antidepressant drug. Well, the drug was progressively making things worse: I was getting "jumpy" and irritable, and didn't realize that those pills were causing more harm than good until I had only one pill left in the bottle! (I threw that one away!)

We must replace thoughts of worry, anxiety, fear etc., with the word of God.

Philippians 4:8 - Finally brethren, whatsoever things are true, whatsoever things are honest, whatsoever things are just; whatsoever things are pure; whatsoever things are lovely; whatsoever things are of good report, if there be any virtue, if there be any praise, think on these things.

You have the choice to choose what you think about, you are to cast down imaginations that are contrary to the word of God and that are contrary to your peace of mind. "Choose: to Refuse Worry"!

Watch what goes into your mind and heart. Beware of too much news, especially 'bad' news!

3. The Prayer of Agreement

Matthew 18:19-20 - Again, I say unto you, that if two of you shall agree on earth as touching anything that they shall ask, it shall be done for them of my Father which is in heaven.

20. For where two or three are gathered together in my name, there am I in the midst of them.

- 'Agree' here means: to be in harmony, to consent, to admit that a thing is true, to sound together, to be in accord, to come to one mind.

So, in the prayer of agreement two (or more) people are "saying" the same thing (in harmony) about a specific thing that they are praying about.

- Once you have prayed and agreed on or about a certain thing you must guard your mind against doubt and unbelief, since you have agreed according to the Word of God, think and act only according to the agreement, and Jesus will go to work to bring it to pass" There am I in the midst of them" Matthew 18:20. He is in the midst of that agreement to bring it to pass.

- The best way to stay 'in touch' and in harmony with your agreement is to write it down, in your prayer book, notebook, etc., where you can see it often and keep your confessions in line with the agreement. Your spirit, soul and actions must agree with your prayer. Agreeing with the word concerning the situation, controlling your mind, not to drift away from thinking only the answer, and acting or preparing for the results will allow God to work on your behalf.

- Harmony is a key word in prayer. Jesus said in Mark 11:25-26, when ye stand praying, forgive if you have ought (anything) against any (anyone) that your Father which is in heaven may forgive you your trespasses, but, if ye do not forgive, neither will your Father which is in heaven forgive your trespasses.

- You must forgive. Be quick to forgive, when you pray. Unforgiveness will cripple your faith. *Faith is what makes prayer work, and faith works by Love, Galatians 5:6. Love is quick to forgive. Don't hold grudges, unforgiveness or anything contrary to harmonizing with God and His word. You cannot fail when you let Love Rule.

- SAMPLE Prayer of Agreement:

Father, In Jesus name, _____ and I see in your word in Matthew 8:17, that Jesus took our infirmities and bore our sicknesses. We are agreeing in prayer according to Matthew 18:19-20 and Matthew 8:17, that this pain, symptom and cause be removed from my body in Jesus name. We believe it's done and we thank you for it. We establish this agreement in Jesus name. Amen

4. The Prayer of Binding and Loosing

Matthew 18:18 – Verily, I say unto you, whatsoever ye shall bind on earth, shall be bound in heaven, and whatsoever ye shall loose on earth, shall be loosed in heaven.

The prayer of binding and loosing is to stop satan in his plans and strategies against the Body of Christ, We have authority over satan in Jesus' name. We are to exercise that authority, by binding him and his forces against hindering us in any way.

EXAMPLE: Satan, I bind you, and command you to stop your attack against us in this situation in Jesus' Name!

- Once you have bound satan, don't give him any place by talking about the problem. Talk only the answer, the word of God. Remember that satan is a defeated foe.

Colossians 2:15 - And having spoiled principalities and powers he made a shew of them openly, triumphing over them in it.

One translation says that God disarmed the principalities that were against us. Through Jesus' work on the cross and His resurrection, we have been given the right to use His name and bind every force that is against us.

- Then, once the devil is bound we have a host of angels, ordained of God to minister on our behalf.

Hebrews 1:14 - (talking about the angels) Are they not all ministering spirits sent forth to minister for them who shall be heirs of salvation?

- We are heirs of salvation and we are to loose these ministering spirits (angels) to work on our behalf: *Ministering spirits, we loose you to minister in our behalf according to the word of God, in Jesus' Name:" NOW, expect them to go to work for you, and again, watch your words!

Negative or contrary words against your faith will stop the angels from working for you. They hearken to words! Psalm 103:20

5.   The Prayer of Petition and Supplication

Philippians 4:6 - Be careful for nothing, but in everything by prayer and supplication with thanksgiving let your requests be made known unto God.

Ephesians 6:18 - Praying always with all prayer and supplication in the Spirit, and watching thereunto with all perseverance and supplication for all saints.

1 Timothy 2:1-2 - I exhort therefore, that, first of all, supplications, prayers, intercessions and giving of thanks, be made for all men;

2.   For kings, and for all that are in authority, that we may lead a quiet and peaceable life in all godliness and honesty.

- Supplication means a formal request of a higher power: a humble, earnest entreaty or request.

Just like the prayer of agreement, we should write out our prayer of supplication, we are to know what God's word says about our petition: This gives us solid ground for believing that God will answer our prayers.

1 John 5:14-15 - And this is the confidence that we have in him, that, if we ask anything according to his will, he heareth us:

15.   And if we know that he hears us, whatsoever we ask, we know that we have the petitions that we desired of Him.

- We make petitions and supplications for ourselves, for those in authority (pastors, teachers, administrators, presidents, congressmen, judges, policemen, employers, employees, etc), and also for all saints, and for all men, including the lost or unsaved.

- What should we pray?

One thing is that "they might be filled with the knowledge of His (God's) will in all wisdom and spiritual understanding." (Colossians 1:9)

- Pray the Lord of the harvest for laborers across the paths of the lost: Matthew 9:37-38.

- Sample Prayer of Petition

Father, In Jesus' Name, according to your word in Matthew 7:7, Ask, and it shall be given you; seek and ye shall find; knock and it shall be opened unto you. I am asking you to supply the resources for this project _____. I receive it and I thank you for it, in Jesus name.

4. 6. United Prayer

United Prayer is when groups of believers gather together to pray, on one accord, to God, the scripture states in Deuteronomy 32:30, that one shall chase a thousand, and two; ten thousand. Believers who gather together on one accord have tremendous power available to them. An example of United Prayer is found in Acts 4:21-31.

So when they had further threatened them, they let them go, finding nothing how they might punish them, because of the people: for all men glorified God for that which was done.

22. For the man was above forty years old, on whom this miracle of healing was shown.

23. And being let go, they went to their own company, and reported all that the chief priests and elders had said unto them.

24. And when they heard that, they lifted up their voice to God with one accord, and said, Lord, thou art God, which hast made heaven, and earth, and the sea, and all that in them is:

25. Who by the mouth of thy servant David has said, Why did the heathen rage, and the people imagine vain things?

26. The kings of the earth stood up, and the rulers were gathered together against the Lord, and against his Christ.

27. For of a truth against thy holy child Jesus, whom thou has anointed, both Herod, and Pontius Pilate, with the Gentiles, and the people of Israel, were gathered together,

28. For to do whatsoever thy hand and thy counsel determined before to be done.

29. And now, Lord, behold their threatening; and grant unto thy servants, that with all boldness they may speak thy word,

30. By stretching forth thine hand to heal: and that signs and wonders may be done by the name of thy holy child Jesus.

31. And when they had prayed, the place was shaken where they were assembled together; and they were all filled with the Holy Ghost, and they spake the word of God with boldness.

- After they prayed together, in one accord, verse 31 says the place was shaken: God came on the scene to answer their prayer!

Psalm 133:1-3 - Behold, how good and how pleasant it is for brethren to dwell together in unity!

2. It is like the precious ointment upon the head, that ran down upon the beard, even Aaron's beard: that went down to the skirts of his garments;

3. As the dew of Hermon, and as the dew that descended upon the mountains of Zion: for there the Lord commanded the blessing, even life for evermore.

How very important it is for us to be on one accord, to be in harmony and be unified against anything that comes against us: "For there the Lord commanded the blessing." Good things happen when we are on one accord!

7. The Prayer of Intercession

1 Timothy 2:1-4 - I exhort therefore, that first of all, supplications, prayers, intercessions, and giving of thanks be made for all men;

2. For kings, and for all that are in authority; that we may lead a quiet and peaceable life in all godliness and honesty.

3. For this is good and acceptable in the sight of God our Saviour;

4. Who will have all men to be saved, and to come unto the knowledge of the truth.

- We intercede for others, that they might be saved, healed, or delivered from any other area the devil might have them in bondage.

- Jesus came to this earth as an intercessor:

Isaiah 59:16-17 - And he saw that there was no man, and wondered that there was no intercessor: therefore his arm brought salvation unto him; and his righteousness, it sustained him.

17. For he put on righteousness as a breastplate, and an helmet of salvation upon his head; and he put on the garments of vengeance for clothing, and was clad with zeal as a cloak.

"His arm" is referring to Jesus. Between man and God he brought reconciliation. We as believers are to take up the ministry of intercession for this lost generation.

- Praying in tongues, or in the Spirit is vitally important in intercessory prayer.

Romans 8:26 - Likewise the Spirit also helpeth our infirmities: for we know not what we should pray for as we ought: but the Spirit itself [Himself] maketh intercession for us with groanings which cannot be uttered.

- We don't know exactly what to pray for, or exactly how to pray for others because we don't know all the details, but the Holy Spirit knows, so by praying in the Spirit, we allow the Holy Spirit to pray the perfect will of God through us for others.

"He maketh intercession for the saints according to the will of God, (Romans 8:27)

- If you are not filled with the Spirit; with the evidence of speaking in tongues, you are missing out on a great benefit of your salvation.

Acts 1:8 - But ye shall receive power after that the Holy Ghost is come upon you: and ye shall be witnesses unto me both in Jerusalem, and in all Judea, and in Samaria and unto the uttermost part of the earth.

- You need power in your life to help you overcome the storms and adversities brought about by evil forces, and the Holy Ghost is that power.

- **To be Filled:**

Luke 11:13 - If ye then, being evil (natural) know how to give good gifts unto your children: how much more shall your heavenly Father give the Holy Spirit to them that ask him? -- So all you need to do is ask, and receive.

*Pray This:

Father, In Jesus Name, as your child, having received Jesus as my Lord and Savior, I realize I need power in my life, so fill me now with your Holy Spirit. I receive him now in Jesus Name. (Then yield your tongue to the Holy Spirit and speak)

Praying in other tongues is of utmost importance when you are interceding about a particular person or thing, because you don't always know the details about the situation, but the Holy Spirit knows, so He joins with us to pray the perfect will of God.

(Romans 8:26) When you pray in tongues you pray beyond your limited understanding, you are also praying in an area where the enemy cannot sabotage your prayer.

- I have prayed in tongues (in the Spirit) for others for several hours at a time* and have witnessed tremendous results!

Ephesians 6:18 - Praying always with all prayer and supplication in the Spirit, and watching thereunto with all perseverance and supplication for all saints;

In **James 5:16** - we are admonished to: "Pray one for another that ye may be healed" – so don't take your prayer life lightly, there is dynamic power in prayer!

- **Also see section on Thanksgiving, Praise and Worship.**

- **Example of Intercessory Prayer for Salvation:**

Father, in Jesus' Name, I pray and intercede for _____.

You spirit of darkness that blinds the mind of _____, I bind you and command you to loose _____ in Jesus' name! Father, you said in your Word in 1 Timothy 2:4 that it is your will that all men be saved, so according to Ephesians 1:17 that you give unto _____ the spirit of wisdom and revelation of you. I claim _____ for the kingdom of God in Jesus' Name – (Then pray in the spirit).

Making the Incurable: Curable - ** By Faith **

Having Faith for Healing

Faith, what is it? How does it work? We have all heard about faith. Some people like to hear about faith, some people don't! Why? Because faith demands action on your part, you have to act like you've got it before you get it, and the natural mind argues with this fact because it doesn't want to look or sound stupid.

So what is faith: Belief in God, revelation or the like; Trust in God; complete confidence, especially in someone or something open to question or suspicion.

Hebrews 11:1 - Now faith is the substance of things hoped for, the evidence of things not seen.

(Evidence: clearness, an outward sign, proof, to bear witness)

Substance: Make-up, material, solidity, reality, resource, *that which underlies all outward manifestations, the unchanging essence or nature of a thing, that which constitutes anything; what it is.

Moffatt: "Now faith means that we are confident of what we hope for, convinced of what we do not see."

NEB – Faith gives substance to our hopes

- Faith is the warranty deed that the things for which we have fondly hoped is at last ours.

- Faith is laying hold of the unrealities of hope, and bringing them into the realm of reality.

- Faith is a spiritual force that brought forth this natural, seen world.

Romans 3:27 - states that faith is a Law, a Law is a set principle, when put to work it has to work.

Every promise that God has given us has the power of faith in itself to cause it to happen, or to come to pass. We have to take that promise, and develop (build) our faith in the promise until the power of the promise gets into our spirits, when that happens we will have the manifestation.

How do you develop faith in a promise, (or in the word)?

1. Believe - that the word is true, the absolute truth.

2. Meditate - think about how that promise changes your situation, see yourself the way the word sees you, (by whose stripes ye were healed) see yourself as 'were' - already healed.

3. Agree - with the word; don't challenge it. If God said it's so, that's final authority! Agree with God.

4. Confess - the word out aloud so that your spirit will pick up what you are saying.

5. Act - like you have it. (don't pay attention to or listen to anything contrary).

    (You might have to turn off all negatives (T.V., News, gossips, street talk, etc.) and turn on Healing scriptures night and day until you see positive results.

6. Decide you will walk in Love. Galatians 5:6 says "Faith worketh by Love" so make sure you are not holding unforgiveness or anything against anyone, and that your heart is right with God. 1 John 1:9 reads: If we confess our sins, He (God) is faithful and just to forgive us our sins, and to cleanse us from all unrighteousness.

** How Faith Works **

You must realize that what you repeatedly (continually) hear, you will eventually believe. That's why Romans 10:17 says, so then faith cometh by hearing, and hearing by the word of God.

Notice: Not by hearing once, but by hearing and hearing, hearing and hearing. Hearing a thing continually is what sparks faith in our hearts.

Why do we need to hear something continually, or (over and over again)?

We must be convinced that what God is saying is true, Romans 4:21, says that Abraham was fully persuaded (absolutely certain, fully convinced, in full assurance, in firm conviction that) God was able to do what he had promised.

What made Abraham convinced? Well the promise to him was that he would become the father of many nations, but the present conditions indicated that was impossible, because he was too old and his wife Sarah was barren. There was no hope! But God did something for him that made him to hope against hope. In other words when all his natural hope was gone, God gave him supernatural hope. How? By changing his name! At the time God made a covenant with him, his name was Abram (potential father), but God changed his name to Abraham (Father of Nations, or a multitude). So every time he heard his name, he saw himself a father of multitudes. He heard it enough until he could 'see' himself a father of multitudes.

- We must be convinced because we have an enemy who will come to challenge our faith. The devil will come against the mind and try to convince you that the word is not true, or that it will not work for you.

This is when you need to be fully persuaded, that what God has said, or promised, he is able to perform.

Now to be fully persuaded we need to follow Abraham's faith by:

- Calling those things that be not as though they were. (Romans 4:17)

- Against hope, believe in hope, when it looks hopeless in the natural. Look only at God's Word which gives supernatural hope. All things are possible to him who believes) Mark 9:23.

- Consider not your body or the circumstances (consider Jesus) who bore your sins and sicknesses in His body, 1-Peter 2:24.

- Don't stagger, (waver or doubt) at the promise through unbelief.

- Be strong in faith, by giving glory to God! Praise Him as if it's already done!

Another way to become fully persuaded is to 'change' your name: by calling yourself what God calls you: Instead of calling yourself sick – call yourself Healed, "I am healed" - I am well - "I am rich" - I am more than a conqueror.

Instead of calling yourself weak, say: " I am strong"!

(**Also see section on 'Confessions brings Possessions"**)

- Remember: What you continually hear, you will eventually believe. You have got to hear, and hear. Keep hearing!

- Faith for salvation comes by hearing the word:

Ephesians 2:8 - For by grace are ye saved through faith, and that not of yourselves, it is the gift of God.

How do you get faith to be saved: Let's go to Romans Chapter 10.

Romans 10:8-10, 13, 17 - But what saith it? The word is nigh thee, even in thy mouth, and in thy heart: that is, the word of faith, which we preach:

9. That if thou shalt confess with thy mouth the Lord Jesus, and shalt believe in thine heart that God hath raised him from the dead, thou shalt be saved.

10.   For with the heart man believeth unto righteousness; and with the mouth confession is made unto salvation.

13.   For whosoever shall call upon the name of the Lord shall be saved.

17.   So then faith cometh by hearing, and hearing by the word of God.

- Faith for salvation comes from hearing words

Acts 11:13-14 - Send men to Joppa and call for Simon, whose surname is Peter, who shall tell thee words whereby thou and all thy house shall be saved.

- Faith for Salvation comes by hearing words.

- How does faith for healing come? The same way, by hearing words.

Acts 14: 7-10 - And there they preached the gospel.

8.   And there sat a certain man at Lystra, impotent in his feet, being a cripple from his mother's womb, who never had walked:

9.   The same heard Paul speak: who steadfastly beholding him, and perceiving that he had faith to be healed,

10.   Said with a loud voice, Stand upright on thy feet. And he leaped and walked.

- **Notice**: this cripple man got faith to be healed when he heard the word that Paul spoke. "And Paul perceived that the man had faith to be healed".

God has provided a way for our every need to be met, and we need to learn how to receive everything He has given us. Faith makes a way. Everything comes by the faith principle: By hearing and hearing.

Faith for finances comes by hearing the word concerning finances such as Luke 6:38 - Give, and it shall be given unto you, good measure, pressed down, shaken together and running over shall men give unto your bosom. By hearing the word and applying the principles, you receive. (In order to receive you are required to give).

Faith for Peace comes by hearing and obeying the Word:

Philippians 4:6-7 - Be careful for nothing; (Don't worry about a thing!) but in everything by prayer and supplication with thanksgiving let your request be made known unto God.

7.   And the peace of God, which passeth all understanding, shall keep your hearts and minds through Christ Jesus.

Faith for healing comes by continually hearing the word on healing, for example 1 Peter 2:24 says, By whose stripes ye were healed. Listen, meditate - 'were' 'were' 'were' - Were means already;

'were' is past tense. Faith says you are already healed. Confess and think about it until you 'see' and possess what you are saying (hearing).

** Faith and Hope **

Hebrews 11:1 - Now faith is the substance of things hoped for.

So what is Hope? Hope is a confident expectation, a happy anticipation - a desire - a dream - a mold - an inner image - a blueprint - a goal setter - an internal picture.

- Where do we get Hope?

Romans 15:4 - For whatsoever things were written aforetime were written for our learning, that we through patience and comfort of the scriptures might have hope.

Acts 26:6 - And now I stand and am judged for the hope of the promise made of God unto our Fathers.

- We see clearly in these two scriptures that hope comes from the scriptures (The Word of God) and from the promises that God made to us through his word.

1-Peter 1:21b - That your faith and hope might be in God. (Primarily, faith in God is faith in His word).

Words create images or pictures on the screen of your heart (spirit), which when received, goes to work to bring to pass a "duplicate" into the physical, natural world - This is the way God operates, (we are made in the image and likeness of God).

- Hope operates in your imagination. You must have an image of the thing you want, or desire. By focusing on that image, you can see 'how' you can have that thing you desire, and what you need to do to get it.

Words trigger a thought (image) and a thought triggers an action and the action triggers results of the things that word defines.

If you can 'see' it, you can have it. Whatever you can imagine on the inside can become a reality on the outside. Someone said, "Imagination rules the world," and someone else said "Imagination is better than knowledge!" Your imagination is a powerful thing! Use it to your advantage. Instead of seeing a situation impossible, imagine the opposite; imagine all things possible!

If you can see it, you can have it! It's like an Easter Egg Hunt. If you don't 'see' anything, you don't get anything! In faith, you look (meditate) until you 'see'! The 'eggs' are out there!

There are no hopeless situations, only people who give up their hope.

Romans 4:18 - says, Abraham against hope believed in hope. He had no natural hope, but he took hold on God's hope, the hope that knows no boundary!

Romans 15:13 - says, God is the God of hope, so as long as there is God, there is hope!

1 Timothy 6:12 - Fight the good fight of faith – If there is a fight there must be an enemy.

Ephesians 6:12 - tells us our enemies are not flesh and blood.

Four Enemies of Faith

1. The greatest enemy (hindrance) to faith is a lack of knowledge. Faith comes by hearing and hearing, when you have a knowledge of God's word, nothing can keep you from receiving. *Knowledge will make you what you want to be. Set yourself to hear, read and meditate.

2. Another enemy to faith is a sense of unworthiness. We all have had a battle with that. Jesus is our worthiness.

1 Corinthians 1:30 - Jesus is made unto us wisdom, righteousness, sanctification and redemption.

Don't look at yourself in the natural, see yourself 'in Him,' a new creature. If you don't see yourself the way God sees you, you will see all your faults, past mistakes, shortcomings, failures, etc.

Many people are not healed, filled with the Holy Spirit, delivered from habits, or have their needs met because they think they don't deserve them.

- It's not what we deserve, it's what God has freely given to us, and it's an insult to Him if we don't receive. We are God-like creatures with god-like qualities and abilities. We are the righteousness of God in Christ Jesus, Corinthians 5:21.

3. The third enemy of faith is accepting substitutes. By just mentally agreeing and not acting on the word you will be prone to accept second best (or worse). Also we can't substitute hope for faith (I'm hoping and praying) - In such cases faith can't work, we need to hope, believe, and pray.

4. The fourth enemy to faith is wavering. James 1:6, Let him ask in faith, nothing wavering. Wavering is doubting: Having a positive confession today, and tomorrow: "I don't know", Boy, It's tough! Once you make your confession: Stand. Having done all to stand: STAND!

- I have often wondered why there are some people who preach against faith or scoffed at the faith message, when Hebrews 11:6 declares that, without faith, it is impossible to please God.

Certainly ignorance, or lack of knowledge plays a big part, but I believe that commitment and responsibility head the list of 'whys'.

In Galatians 1:8 - Paul is saying – But even if we, or an angel from heaven preach any other gospel to you than that we have preached unto you, let him be accursed. Romans 10:8 - the word is nigh thee even in thy heart, and in thy mouth, that is the word of faith which we preach. What is it that he preached? The Word of faith, any other gospel brings a curse.

Some people, especially religious people, when they hear you talk about faith, immediately think about money or things but faith covers all areas of life; all we have to do with in this life. The Bible states in at least four places that the just, (the righteous) shall live by faith (Galatians 3:11; Habbakuk 2:4; Hebrews 10:38, and Romans 1:17. That is an established fact. Out of the mouth of two or three witness let a thing be established, Matthew 18:16; - 2-Corinthians 13:1.

Our lives are to be sustained by our faith in God. The time is coming, and now is, that every believer must begin to 'be' a believer, we must, as individuals learn how faith works and work it! Don't wait until situations get so rough until you have to cry out for help. We live in a violent world where some people don't value life at all: suicides, suicide bombers, robbers, murderers, etc., make the 'uninformed' wonder: "What's the world coming to?"

But we as Christians have the answer - Mark 11:22, Says, Have faith in God, (have the God-kind of faith or have faith like God.) You won't ever see God disturbed about anything. You can't respond in a positive way to anything when you are disturbed or confused. Be cool, and God will show you the way to go.

Here is a great nugget of truth that will do you some good, and inspire you to study and live by faith: Faith allows you to live supernaturally in this natural world! This is God's desire!

Look at Jesus' life (on the earth); He was a flesh and blood man, yet he lived above the forces and things that would cause a person to sink in despair. He was tempted in all points just like we are yet without sin. He used the faith of God to overcome, and he is telling us to use God's faith!

Jesus prayed in Matthew 6:10, Thy will be done in earth, as it is in heaven. Well how do they live in heaven? - In lack? - In trouble? - Sick? We know better! Even though we face trouble on earth, Jesus said, be of good cheer! And we know there is no sickness or shortage in heaven because heaven is the Motherland. Every good gift and every perfect gift is from above, from the Father of light. So, how do they live in heaven? By Faith! 100% Faith! Heaven is lit by faith. Faith is heaven's electricity!

So to please God we must live by faith.

Here are some important things we need to know about faith:

#1. Faith will not work with unforgiveness in your heart.

Mark 11:25-26 - And when ye stand praying, forgive, if you have ought against any; that your Father also which is in heaven may forgive you your trespasses.

26. But if you do not forgive, neither will your Father which is in heaven, forgive you your trespasses. Unforgiveness will stop the faith flow,

Galatians 5:6 says, faith works by Love. Love forgives, and forgets!

Can unforgiveness stop a person from being healed? Certainly, even if you were wronged by someone else, God requires you to forgive. If you want to be forgiven, and who is it among us that is without fault? Holding a grudge or being bitter against someone else doesn't affect them as much as it affects you. Unforgiveness is a 'luxury' you cannot afford! Forgive and Live!

#2. Faith is a spiritual force (a heart force, not a head force)

Faith is not a 'state of mind,' no more than fear is a 'state of mind,' these are real spiritual forces. We humans are spirit beings, we have a soul, and live in a physical body. We can't know God through our minds. You can't reason God in and we can't reason him out. It is by faith in the heart (spirit) that we communicate with God. God is not a mind. God is a Spirit.

John 4:24 - God is a spirit, and they that worship him must worship him in spirit, and in truth.

#3. Heart faith is activated by speaking and acting

You put your faith to work by speaking, and or/acting. Your faith is activated when you speak. Remember we are putting laws into motion when we speak, (whosoever shall say, shall have what-soever he saith. Mark 11:23).

We must remember that words carry power. When we speak, agents are present to hearken and carry out our words, Psalm 103:20 - Bless the Lord ye his angels that excel in strength, that do his commandments, hearkening unto the voice of his Word. We are not to take words lightly. If you speak negative words or things against yourself, there are also agents present to hearken to and carry out your negative words and bring negative things to pass in your life. By your own words!

#4.Faith will work by speaking only, or faith will work in Prayer

Matthew 8:5-8 - And when Jesus was entered into Capernaum there came unto him a centurion, beseeching him.

6. And saying, Lord, my servant lieth at home sick of the palsy, grievously tormented,

7. And Jesus saith unto him, I will come and heal him,

8. The Centurion answered and said, Lord, I am not worthy that thou shouldest come under my roof: but speak the word only, and my servant shall be healed.

(The Centurion went on to say that he understood the authority of words.)

In Acts 3 - Peter spoke words to the cripple man, and the man was healed.

Acts 14 - Paul spoke to the impotent man at Lystra (He perceived that the man had faith to be healed) and he said, "Stand upright on thy feet" and he leaped and walked.

In Prayer:

John 11:41 - Jesus prayed and spoke (concerning Lazarus). He prayed to the Father, "Father I thank you that thou hast heard me' then He said; Lazarus, come forth!

In Acts 9:36 - Peter kneeled down and prayed, and Tabitha was healed.

So Faith works both ways *By saying, *whosoever shall say, shall have whatsosever he saith. *By Praying: When you pray, believe you receive and you shall have it.

#5. You can have faith in your faith

Your faith, that, you have taken the time to build and develop will always work for you. Many times you can use your faith to help others but your faith is your key to the blessings of heaven. It is time for every Christian to get in the word of God and build and develop a strong faith for himself or herself.

You cannot expect to ride on someone else's faith all the time. There won't be someone else around all the time to get you out of your "jam". Read, study, meditate and confess the word until it gets into your spirit. There is something about knowing what you know! Meditate (think about) the scripture that says "By whose stripes ye were healed". Ponder in your heart: "were" is past tense! That means you are already healed. Anything contrary to "were" must leave!

No one can stop your faith from working but you. Nobody can! God won't, and the devil can't. James 4:7 says, submit yourselves therefore to God (the Word), resist the devil, and he will flee from you.

So, study and apply the principles of faith, and remember that, "faith allows you to live supernaturally in this natural world." God wants you to ride on His faith. Believe and receive. 1-John 5:4 – This is the victory that overcomes the world, even our faith.

More "Gems" About Faith:

- Faith is your Victory
- Whatever you want from God you must receive by Faith
- Faith believes in things it does not see
- Faith changes hope into reality
- Faith acts in the face of contrary circumstances
- Faith counts things done: Before God Acts!
- Faith knows it's done!
- Faith is your energy. Faith is to your spirit, what gasoline is to your car!

- Faith is heaven's electricity

- Faith is your life (the just shall live by faith)

- Faith is what makes your dreams come true!

- Faith is the only known cure for failure!

- (In this life): Faith is your vehicle (faith takes you where you want to go!)

- Faith makes the unobtainable: obtainable

- Faith makes the impossible: POSSIBLE

- Faith makes the incurable: CURABLE

- Finale: Faith is the Substance of everything you will ever need!

Making the Incurable: Curable

HINDRANCES and ROADBLOCKS to HEALING

Roadblock #1- The thought that it might not be God's will to heal you.

God's word is His will. He has provided total redemption for us as outlined in **Isaiah 53:4-5**:

4. Surely, he hath borne our griefs, and carried our sorrows, yet we did esteem him stricken, smitten of God and afflicted.

5. But, He was wounded for our transgressions, he was bruised for our iniquities: The chastisement of our peace was upon him: and with his stripes we are healed.

1. Spirit: He was wounded for our transgressions, bruised for our iniquities (*He paid the price for our sins).

2. Soul: The Chastisement of our peace was upon him. (He suffered mental torment for us so that we don't have to.

3. Body: Surely he hath borne our griefs (Literal: sickness and disease) and carried our sorrows (pains).

- Literal Hebrew: Surely He hath lifted, carried our borne, our sicknesses, diseases and our pains.

God's word is His Will. If you want to know the perfect will of God in regards to healing, look at the ministry of Jesus in the Gospels. About one third of His ministry was spent in healing the sick. You cannot find one instant where a sick person approached Him for healing and He turned them down. Jesus was the will of God in action, and he is the same yesterday, today and forever, Hebrews 13:8.

John 6:38 - For I came down from heaven, not to do mine own will, but the will of Him that sent me.

In Luke 5:12-13 - Jesus was approached by a man full of leprosy, who said unto Jesus: Lord, if thou wilt, thou canst make me clean, and He (Jesus) put forth his hand and touched him saying, I will, be thou clean, and immediately the leprosy departed from him.

3 John 2 - Beloved, I wish above all things that thou mayest prosper *and be in health, even as thy soul prospereth.

Tradition and religion will rob a person of these truths, especially when they have been taught that "everybody gets sick sometimes" or "healing isn't for everybody" or "I'm just suffering for Jesus".

Several years ago a woman, a preacher's wife, had open-heart surgery to repair some blockages, etc. I often would visit her and give her scriptures, healing tapes and pray for her, however, she couldn't shake the "if it be thy will" thing. Well, the last time I visited, her nurse was there and examined her thoroughly and said she was recuperating well. After praying with her and giving some encouraging words, she replied (just before I left), "Well, if it is God's will I'll make it through, if not, I'll go on home." Exactly one week later, she was gone! I can't help but think that her words took her on out!

1 Peter 2:24 - Who his own self bare our sins in his own body on the tree that we, being dead to sins should live unto righteousness, by whose stripes ye were healed.

- If you see it in the Word, you have heard from God!

Roadblock #2- Sin

Sin (missing the mark or transgressing God's Laws) could very well be the major block or hindrance to healing; however, sin will not stop a person from being healed if that person will repent and turn to God.

James 5:15 - And the prayer of faith shall save (or heal) the sick and the Lord shall raise him up; and if he has committed sins, they shall be forgiven him.

- True repentance always lead to healing
- Jesus told the man in John 5:14 - Behold, thou art made whole: sin no more lest a worse thing come upon thee.

Roadblock #3- Doubt and Unbelief

Doubt and unbelief is caused mainly by religious tradition, which programs a person to believe things contrary to the word of God. And even faced with the truth, doubt or unbelief springs up.

In Mark 7:13 and Matthew 15:6 - Jesus said that the people had made the Word of God of None effect (ineffective to work on their behalf) because of their traditions.

Matthew 13:58 and Mark 6:5-6 - states that in Nazareth, [Jesus] could do no mighty works there because of their unbelief.

- Doubt is a thief, and will stop the power from flowing in your life.

Healing does not fall on people automatically, any more than salvation comes automatically. These things operate by Laws. Faith is a Law. Faith comes by hearing and hearing by the Word of God. Healing comes by hearing and hearing the word on healing and receiving by faith.

Roadblock #4- Basing your Faith on Someone Else's Experience

"So and so was prayed for, and they didn't get healed". Never base your faith on someone else's experience; look to God's word. You don't know what's in the life of another person, (it could be some 'secret sin' that's hindering them like, unforgiveness, malice, etc.). You have to get in the word and believe God for yourself.

Roadblock #5- I'm Sick for the Glory of God

Here again is a religious tradition. What pleasure do you get out of seeing another person sick or crippled, or diseased? If you have the least compassion, you would want to see that person well.

God is compassion; He is Love, and Psalm 35:27b says:

Let the Lord be magnified, which hath pleasure in the prosperity of his servant. One translation says, "Who delights in the welfare of His servant! (RSV)

God is glorified when we are healed. John 9:1-7 - Jesus healed the blind man saying that "The works of God was being manifested in him." The 'works of God' is healing. Sickness came as a result of the fall of man. God sent redemption through Jesus to heal us.

- There are actually some people who 'enjoy' bad health. In reality, they enjoy the pampering, and the attention they get from sympathizing people.

Roadblock #6- Sickness is God's Chastening

Some believe that God is chastising them with sickness because of some wrong they have done. This erroneous teaching have cost many their lives! God is a spirit, you are a spirit; when he chastises, he does so through His word: The words that I speak unto you they are spirit, and they are life, John 6:63.

2 Timothy 3:16 - All scripture is given by inspiration of God and is profitable for doctrine, reproof, for correction, for instruction in righteousness. Reproof, correction and instruction are all the chastening God does, any other 'chastening' comes from some other source!"

Roadblock# 7- Violating Natural Laws

Bad diet, bad habits such as alcohol, drugs, tobacco, etc, and a lack of knowledge of certain things can be detrimental to your health.

(See section on "Obeying NATURAL LAWS")

Making the Incurable: Curable

Steps to Receive Healing

Step #1- Use The Name Of Jesus

Philippians 2:9-11 - Wherefore God also hath highly exalted him, and given him a name which is above every name:

10. That at the name of Jesus every knee should bow, of things in heaven, and things in earth, and things under the earth;

11. And that every tongue should confess that Jesus Christ is Lord, to the glory of God the Father.

Mark 16:17 - And these signs shall follow them that believe; In my name shall they cast out devils.

Use the Name of Jesus against the devil. Demand in the name of Jesus that the sickness or disease leave.

We have a right to use the Name of Jesus. There is power in the name of Jesus.

Step #2- Pray for Healing to the Father in Jesus' Name

John 16:23 - And in that day ye shall ask me nothing, whatsoever ye shall ask the Father in my name, He will give it you.

Step #3- AGREE in PRAYER

Matthew 18:19-20 - And again I say unto you, that if two of you shall agree on earth as touching anything that they shall ask, it shall be done for them of my Father which is in heaven.

20. For where two or three are gathered together in my name, there am I in the midst of them.

• Find someone who will agree with you in faith, and pray the prayer of agreement, Jesus said, "There am I in the midst of them." (To carry out the agreement!).

Several years ago my dad was suffering from a back ailment, and was almost bowed over when he walked, or was standing. I had prayed for him, but several days after, he was still hovering in pain. I asked another believer to agree with me in prayer, as we prayed, he commanded the devil to "get off dad's back," by the next day he was healed and was walking normally! *There is Power in Agreement.

Step #4- Anoint with Oil

James 5:14-15 - Is any sick among you? Let him call for the elders of the church; and let them pray over him, anointing him with oil in the Name of the Lord,

15.   And nthe prayer of faith shall save the sick, and the Lord shall raise him up.

We must realize that the anointing oil serves only as a symbol, or point of contact to get the sick person to release their faith.

Step #5- Receive Healing through the Laying on of Hands

Mark 16:17-18 - And these signs shall follow them that believe, In my name shall they cast out devils - They shall lay hands on the sick, and they shall recover.

Again, the laying on hands serve as a point of contact to release your faith for healing. When hands are laid on you, believe that you are healed at that moment (regardless of how you feel or what you see) when you release your faith, healing begins at that moment, but it begins on the inside, and is manifested on the outside.

Step #6- Receive Healing through the Gifts of the Spirit

1 Corinthians 12:9 - says one of the spiritual gifts that God has placed in the church is the 'Gifts of Healings'. It is a supernatural manifestation of God's power to heal, transferred from the anointed person to the sick and affecting a cure. These signs are not always in manifestation, but faith in God's word will always work. A person might also be healed or delivered through some of the other gifts, such as the gift of Faith, and the working of miracles.

Step#7- Know that Healing Belongs to You

The best way to receive healing is to know for yourself that healing belongs to you. By studying, reading, listening to the scriptures on healing, meditating on healing scriptures, until you are fully persuaded that Jesus bore your sins in his body on the tree, that you, being dead to sins should live unto righteousness, and by his stripes ye (you) Were healed. Healing belongs to you just as much as salvation belongs to you. Jesus paid it all.

- Again, Remember - Healing sometimes comes by degrees, it is not always instant. Continue in the word, hold fast your confession.
- Praise! Praise! Praise Him.
- Give thanks continually.
- Continual Praise brings God on the Scene!

There is Power in Praise

Psalm 92:1-2 - It is a good thing to give thanks unto the Lord, and to sing praises unto thy name, O most High.

2. To show forth thy loving kindness in the morning, and thy faithfulness every night,

Psalm 8:1-2 - O Lord, our Lord, how excellent is thy name in all the earth! Who hast set thy glory above the heavens,

2. Out of the mouth of babes and sucklings hast thou ordained strength (praise) because of thine enemies, that thou mightest still the enemy and the avenger.

Psalm 9:1-3 - I will praise thee, O Lord, with my whole heart; I will show forth all thy marvelous works.

2. I will be glad and rejoice in thee: I will sing praise to thy name, O thou most High.

3. When mine enemies are turned back, they shall fall and perish at thy presence.

1 Thessalonians 5:16-18 - Rejoice evermore.

17. Pray without ceasing.

18. In every thing give thanks: for this is the will of God in Christ Jesus concerning you.

- Define: Praise, Thanksgiving

Praise: commendation, approbation, to laud, approbation: (act of approving), - to express approval, to magnify, especially in song, acclaim, to give honor.

Thanksgiving, Thanks, Thankful

Thank: kindly or grateful thought, gratitude, grace, favor, an acknowledgement.

Thanksgiving: a prayer expressing gratitude, act of rendering thanks, esp. to God, a public acknowledgement or celebration of divine goodness and mercies.

There is mighty, dynamic power in praise! Psalm 8:2 says, out of the mouth of babes and sucklings (children) God has ordained (or ordered) strength, strength is translated praise.

- Why Praise?

To still, or to stop the enemy and the avenger; to silence revengeful words and plots against you. We see here how praise alone can bring you victory!

Psalm 22:3 – But thou art holy, O thou that inhabitest the praises of Israel.

This verse tells us that God inhabits, or come down and makes His presence known when His people praise Him. His presence will show up in our midst. Why? To stop our enemies - whether the enemy is sickness or disease, lack, debt, fear or a manifestation of demonic or satanic force, praise is ordained by God to bring a halt to the enemy, or whatever is against you. When it seems like there is no answer, Praise to God is a way to hear from God because He is the same yesterday, today, and forever. What He did in the past for His people, He will do in the present.

2 Chronicles 20 tells us of a situation that Jehoshaphat the king was in: Three armies had gathered themselves against Jehoshaphat to battle (They were greatly outnumbered).

A great multitude had gathered against them, and the Bible says that Jehoshaphat feared, (v3) and set himself to seek the Lord. They prayed, they fasted, and they waited upon God. In verse 14, the Spirit of the Lord came upon Jahaziel, a Levite of the sons of Asaph (A worshipper) and told them what to do: *Set yourselves, stand ye still and see the salvation, (or deliverance) of the Lord *for the battle is not yours, but God's! Then God told them what to do: appoint singers and praisers that would praise the beauty of holiness and to say, "Praise the Lord, for His mercy endures forever"!

When they began to sing and praise, the Lord set ambushments against their enemies and they were smitten. They were put in confusion and began to kill one another in their own camp! Praise is a mighty weapon!

- In the New Testament we read the account of the ten lepers, who cried out to Jesus for mercy:

Luke 17:12-19 - And as he entered into a certain village, there met him ten men that were lepers, which stood afar off:

13. And they lifted up their voices, and said, Jesus, Master, have mercy on us.

14. And when he saw them, he said unto them, Go show yourselves unto the priest. And it came to pass, that, as they went, they were cleansed.

15. And one of them, when he saw that he was healed, turned back, and with a loud voice glorified God,

16. And fell down on his face at his feet, giving him thanks: and he was a Samaritan.

17. And Jesus answering said, Were there not ten cleansed? But where are the nine?

18. There are not found that returned to give glory to God, save this stranger.

19. And he said unto him, Arise, go thy way: thy faith hath made thee whole.

These ten men had leprosy: (an infectious disease of the skin, marked by formations of ulcers, nodules or deformities). They cried out to Jesus for mercy, (For Jesus to do something about their conditions). Jesus told them to: "Go show yourselves to the priest," and as they went, (They obeyed Jesus' word,) they were cleansed (healed). Verse 15, and one of them, when he saw he was cleansed, or healed, turned back, and with a loud voice glorified God. He praised God at the top of his voice, and fell down at Jesus' feet and gave him thanks. Jesus answered, were there not ten cleansed? Where are the nine? – And he said to him, arise, go thy way, thy faith hath made thee whole. Whole: He was restored to soundness. all of his deteriorated parts were restored! Look what praise will do!

A well known healing evangelist has told the story numerous times how praise to God brought about healing and strength to his body, weakened by the effects of tuberculosis. He was determined to Praise God until he was completely healed or either die. He began with a whisper, but being determined, the volume of that whisper turned into a loud voice to God: He was healed!

There were times when I had to stand on the word of God and praise God with a loud voice until those attacks of the enemy were defeated.

During a time of prayer and fasting and consecration for several days, one morning I woke up with a swollen gland on the neck, then a thought came to me that, that gland was swollen because I had not eaten in several days; ---- and so on and on went the lie. Well, I entertained that thought for a while, until the pain got almost unbearable. Then the Lord began to warn me to stand on the scriptures, so after reading a few scriptures and expecting a change, I was prompted to praise God - and praise I did! Because that condition was painful, and seemed a threat to my well being, I praised God with a loud voice for about two hours until the swelling subsided right then and there, even though I experienced a slight pain for a day or two afterwards.

I am convinced that praise will stop the enemy in your life and circumstances. It is a good thing to give thanks unto the Lord and to sing praises to the Most High!

Psalm 8:2 - says that the praise of God's people will stop the enemies' attacks, now in Psalm 9:1-3, we see that praise will bring God on the scene and cause our enemies to turn back, fall, and perish at the presence of God. God inhabits (indwells) the praises of His people!

So, always be thankful, no matter what happens, don't let anyone or anything steal your joy, for the joy of the Lord is your strength.

Psalm 136:1 - O give thanks unto the Lord, for He is good: for his mercy endureth forever. Continually praising and thanking God gives you the assurance that His mercy, His help, His providence, His great compassion is always available.

** There is Healing Power in Praise!! **

Worship

Worship: to make obeisance, do reverence to, act of homage or reverence to God, to revere with feeling of awe or devotion, to honor, to serve, to show piety, to do service to, to acknowledge, to give glory to God, intense love or admiration, respect.

While Praise and Thanksgiving is an act, worship is an attitude. Worship should be a part of our nature, once you know God, and all that He is, and all that He has done for us, an attitude of worship should become 'second' nature with us.

Proverbs 3:5-6 - Trust in the Lord with all your heart; and lean not unto your own understanding v6, In all thy ways acknowledge Him, and He shall direct thy paths.

These verses in Proverbs 3:5-6 reveal to us a sure way to be victorious in life. Everything we do, wherever we go, if we would acknowledge God, we have His guarantee that He will direct our paths, (even though it might not be smooth, all the time, or to our liking) we can be assured that God will bring us to a desired end.

"To acknowledge in all thy ways" means to be mindful of, or to have God in mind at all times whether at work, at home, in public, at school, church or wherever you are, you are aware of His presence, you are "God conscious" or "God inside minded" - you sense His presence, and whatever you do, you are mindful of pleasing Him, or, doing those things that are pleasing in his sight. (1st John 3:22) To acknowledge means also to confess, as to own; to perceive, to have full knowledge of.

A true worshipper is one who is aware of God's presence at all times and seeks to please him. Philippians 3:3, for we are the circumcision, which worship God in the spirit and rejoice in Christ Jesus, and have no confidence in the flesh.

John 4:24 - God is a Spirit, and they that worship Him must worship Him in Spirit and in truth.

Actually, we are worshipping God when we honor his word ("Thy word is truth" John 17:17) Let us stand on the word, and bring honor to Him! "By whose stripes ye were healed."

CHAPTER FIVE

Obeying Natural Laws

In obeying natural laws we must realize that our confessions, things we say, go into our spirits, and, in turn affect our bodies. How many times have we heard someone say, "I know I shouldn't eat this, but…, and then they go ahead and eat it anyway. I believe that they are causing more harm to themselves by saying one thing and doing something contrary, than if they would say, "I'm gonna eat this, and it won't hurt me." Just by saying something contrary to what you are doing can cause adverse reactions in your system. The best thing to do is to pray for an alternative, remembering that there is always something better, especially than that which is not good for your health! *Watch your confessions, because you have what you say!

When we understand that everything in this universe operates by law, and not by luck, or chance, we will be more aware of our responsibility to take control of our own lives. Your body operates under natural laws. It requires food, certain nutrients, vitamins and minerals to sustain it, it needs water and air, and it needs rest and movement, (exercise) when any of these things are denied, then a natural law is violated, and it may produce health issues.

Certain foods and nutrients supply the various organs of the body with the necessary elements to function properly, so we need a variety of foods, supplements and nutrients to fuel the many organs, tissues, cells, etc., of the body.

The United States Department of Agriculture (USDA) has given us a chart of the essential foods the body needs. The chart comes in a pyramid with the least essential on the top, such as fats, oils, sweets and 'junk food'. There are many people in America who stay on the top of the pyramid, and wonder why they are experiencing health problems. It is simple: They are violating natural laws.

MAKING THE INCURABLE: CURABLE

Someone said years ago that the average American is killing himself with a high fat, high cholesterol diet. We must become serious with ourselves concerning our health, and do all we can to correct many of the problems we face. We cannot control our appetites, habits, desires, etc., with natural means.

Our bad eating and gluttonous habits are controlled by spiritual forces, so are habits such as drugs, alcoholism, and smoking or using tobacco. How many people die every year of cirrhosis of the liver, simply because they couldn't break the alcohol habit? How many die of lung, throat, mouth cancer or emphysema because they couldn't break the tobacco habit? There are multiplied thousands! Many of them would be alive today if they knew how. As Christians, we don't have any excuse! In Hosea 4:6, God says, "My people are destroyed for lack of knowledge". Knowledge of natural and spiritual laws will keep us from being destroyed. Galatians 5:22 - But the fruit of the spirit is love, joy, peace, longsuffering (patience), gentleness, goodness, faith, meekness, temperance, against such there is no law.

-- (See chapter one: The Two Major Laws) --

We are to control natural habits with spiritual means. By developing faith in the love of God and applying the fruit or force called temperance, (or self control), we can overcome any problem. Against these spiritual forces, of love, joy, peace, temperance, etc., there is NO law. The law of the spirit of life Rules!

Romans 8:22 - For the Law of the Spirit of life in Christ Jesus hath made me free from the law of sin and death.

We as Christians, must take control of our habits and desires, and make them line up with The Word of God.

2 Corinthians 10:5: Casting down imaginations (of over indulging, etc.), and every high thing that exalts itself against the knowledge of God, and bringing into captivity every thought to the obedience of Christ.

It takes continual practice to train your body and your mind to be under control, but it's worth the effort.

Keeping The Body Under

1 Corinthians 9:25, 27

25.   and every man that striveth for the mastery is temperate in all things (practices self control).

27.   But I keep my body under and bring it into subjection: Lest that by any means, when I have preached to others, I myself should be a castaway.

1 Corinthians 6:19-20

19.   What? Know ye not that your body is the temple of the Holy Ghost which is in you, which you have from God, and ye are not your own?

20.   For ye are bought with a price: therefore glorify God in your body and in your spirit, which are God's.

1 Corinthians 6:13b

Now the body is not for fornication, but for the Lord; and the Lord for the body.

James 3:2,6

For in many things we offend all. If any man offend not in word, the same is a perfect man, and able also to bridle the whole body. (If you can control your tongue, you can control your whole body)!

James 3:3-6

3.   Behold, we put bits into the horses' mouths, that they may obey us; and we turn about their whole body.

4.   Behold also the ships, which though they be so great, and are driven about with fierce winds, yet they are turned about with a very small helm, whithersoever the governor listeth (wherever the pilot wants it to go).

5.   Even so the tongue is a little member, and boasteth great things. Behold how great a matter a little fire kindleth.

6.   And the tongue is a fire, a world of iniquity; so is the tongue among our members that it defiles the whole body and sets on fire the course of nature and it is set on fire of hell.

These verses of scripture in James chapter three tell us where trouble in the body comes from. "If any man offend not in word" (If anyone does not speak against his body) he is a mature man and able to control his whole body. Here again, we see a law in motion, temptations to sin, be sick, accept disease, etc., comes to you in the form of suggestions. What you say will be your outcome. If you can control your tongue, you can control your body!

James 3:8 - But the tongue can no man tame, it is an unruly evil, full of deadly poison.

The tongue is set on fire by spiritual forces and must be brought under control by spiritual forces.

James 3:17 - But the wisdom that is from above is first pure, then peaceable, gentle, easy to be entreated, full of mercy and good fruits without partiality and without hypocrisy.

The wisdom of God is the Word of God, so by the Word of God, we can control, or tame the tongue (Speak only what the Word says about it).

Romans 12:1-2

1. I beseech you therefore, brethren, by the mercies of God that ye present your bodies a living sacrifice, holy, acceptable unto God, which is your reasonable service.

2. And be not conformed to this world, but be ye transformed by the renewing of your mind, that ye may prove what is the good, and acceptable, and perfect will of God.

A renewed mind is a mind controlled by the Word of God. Your tongue is directly connected to your spirit, and what's on your mind you speak. Spiritual law says you have what you say.

What you say, everything you say, demands response from a spiritual law.

If you speak words of life; the Law of the Spirit of Life responds, if you speak words contrary to life giving forces, the law of sin and death responds. What you say, for, or against your body, you will eventually experience.

So, be quick to choose words of life: words of love, joy, peace, longsuffering, gentleness, goodness, faith, meekness, temperance , against such, there is no law. Galatians 5:22-23

For the Law of the Spirit of Life in Christ Jesus hath made me free from the law of sin and death.

Romans 8:2 - There is nothing satan, the world, or any other creature can do against you when you are living (walking) under these life giving forces – (love, joy, peace, etc.)

1 Corinthians 6:19 - What? Know you not that your body is the temple of the Holy Ghost? Which is in you, which you have of God, and ye are not your own? Therefore glorify God in your body.

How can we glorify God in our bodies?

1. Obey the scriptures (concerning your body)

   (eg.) 1 Corinthians 3:17 says if any man defile the temple of God, him shall God destroy.

   Things like alcohol, illegal drugs (and some legal), tobacco and many other addictions defile the body, making it unfit for the service of God.

   1 Corinthians 6:18 - flee fornication (which is sin against your own body).

2. Proper Diet: (see the updated nutrition chart)@USADA.org and other sources on Google or YouTube.

   • It is a fact that many of our health problems are diet related.

3. Exercise - (The body needs movement for circulation).

   I Timothy 4:8 - Bodily exercise profits little (has some value).

a) Get Proper Rest - (Even Jesus took time from his busy schedule to rest). (see Mark 6:31)

b) Abstain - from bad substances like alcoholic beverages, illegal drugs (and some legal) tobacco, etc. Bad habits such as gluttonous living (excessive addictions are enforced by evil spirits.)

Hosea 4:6 - "My people are destroyed for lack of knowledge."

Remember that knowledge of natural and spiritual laws will keep us from perishing, (from being destroyed).

We are spirit beings, we possess a soul, and we live in a physical body. All three areas of our being need to be fed and nourished and given proper attention for us to be whole, (sound and operating at peak performance).

1. The Spirit (the real you) needs spiritual food, (The Word of God, when assimilated it produces Faith).

2. The Soul (your mind, will, emotions) needs intellectual (or mental) food (information, instructions, revelations) and produces a power force called will power.

3. The Body needs physical food, when assimilated and put into action, it produces a power called strength.

All these areas must work together for you to be at your best.

Stress and It's Effect on Good Health

Extensive research on stress has found that stress directly affects the immune response, and the body's ability to control bacteria and certain diseases. Individuals experiencing unhappiness or continual dissatisfaction, or stressful situations, usually have a depressed immune system, resulting in illness or a breakdown in the integrated system (spirit, soul and body).

When there is substantial stress, the nervous system shuts down. This results in shutting down the digestive processes, which can lead not only to emotional problems, but to physical ones as well.

Over 75 Super Stress Stoppers

Stopping stress in your life can be a major blessing to your good health. Here are some super stress stoppers:

- Praise God
- Give Thanks – always be thankful "Thank You Lord"!

- Dance a jig! Dancing is good therapy, good exercise as well!

- Find a quiet place and turn on your imagination: Play a mental movie in your mind: See yourself where you want to be. IMAGINE!

- See yourself winning: with God, you can't lose!

- Make Positive Confessions: "I'm free from stress: "I'm free from worries" "I'm free from fear".

- Have a Positive outlook on life, there is Hope: God is the God of hope - Romans 15:13.

- Make a list of your daily activities: most important ones first. GO!

- Take a deep breath – say, "I'm breathing in confidence, I'm breathing out fear!"

- Sing a Song – Sing psalms, hymns, spiritual songs, making melody in your heart to the Lord.

- Exercise – 15-30 minutes daily – walking is great – stretch.

- Eat Right – stay mostly on the bottom of the pyramid (nutrition chart).

- Call a friend.

- Make Friends - A man that hath friends must show himself friendly - Proverbs 18:24.

- Laugh at situations - While we look not at things which are seen - 2 Corinthians 4:18.

- Set realistic goals - Don't bite off more than you can chew.

STRESS STOPPERS

- Take Breaks - Don't wear yourself out.

- Prioritize Tasks - Most important, Less Important, Least Important.

- Delegate Work.

- Avoid clutter - Get organized.

- Use proper lighting - Don't strain your eyes.

- Have a hobby: Good therapy for the soul.

- Keep noise down.

- Learn to relax.

- Take a deep breath - Inhale – Exhale.

- Talk things out.

- Budget time and money.

- Massage tense muscles.

- Reward yourself.

- Set limits.

- Think Positively - Stay Positive.

- Count down 10 - 0: then say "I'm free".

- Say: "I walk by faith, not by sight".

- Avoid junk foods - snack on fruits and vegetables.

- Do neck rolls.

- Practice teamwork - (1) can chase a thousand (2), ten thousand!

- Have faith in God - Trust and Obey.

- Believe in others.

- Believe in yourself - "I can do all things through Christ." Philippians 4:13.

- Enjoy small pleasures.

- Be kind - Treat everyone you meet as the most important person on the earth!

- Laugh! - Good medicine!

- Take a deep breath - Exhale slowly.

- Remember - With God, you can't lose!

- Remember - Time heals.

- Have regular checkups.

- Take a walk - good exercise.

- Get organized: Helps to have a better outlook on life.

- Be flexible.

STRESS STOPPERS

- Avoid bad drugs.

- Stretch often.

- Control your weight.

- Avoid distractions.

- Don't sweat the small stuff.

- Learn to say 'NO': "To the wrong thing at the right time!"

- Forgive and forget: Very important – Don't hold anything against anyone.

- Use the right tools → less strain, better performance.

- Don't procrastinate - do it now! - There is always something you can do.

- Reflect on your joys.

- Encourage others: get your mind off your problems and help others.

- Always be joyful: Even if you have to "fake it"!

- Get up earlier, plan a good day.

- Read - Read - Read: Read the Word - Read good books.

- Break up monotony: Do some things differently.

- Love others: love thy neighbor as thyself.

- Love yourself: Confess "I-Like-Me".

- See problems as challenges - 1 Corinthians 10:15 - There hath no temptation taken you but such as is common to man - God is faithful. Problems are opportunities to advance!

- Stop, smell the roses.

- Screen your calls.

- Avoid unnecessary meetings.

- Give hugs cheerfully.

- Accept hugs - with a smile.

- Seek positive people - *Stay away from grumblers and complainers.

- Be Faithful - be committed to something good - To God, to church, to your family, to your organization.

The Rewards of Fasting

Matthew 6:16-18 - Moreover, when you fast, be not as the hypocrites, of a sad countenance, for they disfigure their faces, that they may appear unto men to fast, verily I say unto you, they have their reward, but thou, when thou fastest, anoint your head, and wash your face that you appear not unto men to fast, but unto thy Father which is in secret: and thy Father, which sees in secret shall reward you openly.

This eighteenth verse says that when we fast with the right motive, God will reward us openly.

- First of all, lets define fasting or fast:

Fast: - to abstain from food; to eat sparingly, or to abstain from certain foods, to practice abstinence as a religious exercise, voluntary abstinence from food.

- There are many variations of fasting, but all of them, when done properly or with the right motive will result in a reward, or benefit.

- Fasting does not change God, it changes you, it puts you in position to receive benefits in three areas: spirit, soul, and body.

Spiritually, fasting shuts done the influence of natural and visible things so that you are more in-tune with and more aware of the spiritual. The world at large, doesn't know that a spiritual world exist. There are many Christians who are not conscious of the spiritual as they should be. Fasting helps us to receive from God, but the fasting itself doesn't move God. Faith in God's Word gets God to move on our behalf. Spiritual rewards include *answers to prayer, a closer walk with God, *divine revelation, *wisdom and insight, and a better understanding of spiritual things.

Note: You must also be aware of evil spirits that will attempt to steer you off course with false prophesy, visions and like things that are not scriptural. The Word of God is a must during a fast. Always base your prayers, fasting, and all spiritual affairs on the Word of God.

- Great healings and deliverances have come about as a result of fasting, as fasting or setting aside a time to seek God in His Word opens the door for a stronger faith and deeper understanding of the spiritual and how it relates to our natural, physical circumstances. Fasting puts you in a position to hear and receive from God.

Fasting can actually be life changing in many different ways, especially when done according to the Word of God. Our fasting is not to impress God, or other people - Matthew 6:16 - moreover when ye fast, be not as the hypocrites, of a sad countenance, or to look sullen or "super spiritual" to show that you are going without food or that you have great self control so that people may praise you. If you fast for that reason, the praise you receive from others will be all the reward you will get. The 58th chapter of Isaiah gives us a list of rewards of fasting when done with the right motive.

Isaiah 58

Cry aloud, spare not, lift up thy voice like a trumpet, and show my people their transgressions, and the house of Jacob their sins.

2. Yet ye seek me daily, and delight to know my ways, as a nation that did righteousness, and forsook not the ordinances of justice; ye take delight in approaching to God.

3. Wherefore have we fasted, say they, and thou seeth not? Wherefore have we afflicted our souls, and thou taketh no knowledge? Behold, in the day of your fast ye find pleasure, and exact all your labors.

4. Behold ye fast for strife and debate, and to smite with the fist of wickedness: ye shall not fast as ye do this day, to make your voice to be heard on high.

5. Is it such a fast that I have chosen? a day for a man to afflict his soul? Is it to bow down thy head as a bulrush, and to spread sackcloth and ashes under him? Wilt thou call this a fast, and an acceptable day to the Lord?

6. Is not this the fast that I have chosen? to loose the bands of wickedness, *to undo the heavy burdens, *and to let the oppressed go free, *and that ye break every yoke?

7. Is it not to deal thy bread to the hungry, and that thou bring the poor that are cast out to thy house? When thou seeth the naked that thou cover him, and that thou hide not thyself from thine own flesh?

8. Then shall thy light break forth as the morning, and *thine health shall spring forth speedily, and *thy righteousness shall go before thee, *the glory of the Lord shall be thy rereward.

9. Then shalt thou call, and the Lord shall answer, thou shalt cry, and He shall say, Here I am, If thou take away from the midst of thee the yoke, the putting forth of the finger and speaking vanity.

10. And if thou draw out thy soul to the hungry, and satisfy the afflicted soul; then shall thy light rise in obscurity, and thy darkness be as the noonday.

11. And the Lord shall guide thee continually, and satisfy thy soul in drought, and make fat thy bones; and thou shalt be like a watered garden, and like a spring of water, whose waters fail not.

12. And they that shall be of thee shall build the old waste places: thou shalt raise up the foundations of many generations, and thou shalt be called the repairer of the breach, the restorer of paths to dwell in.

13. If thou turn away thy foot from the Sabbath, from doing thy pleasure on my holy day, and call the Sabbath a delight, the holy of the Lord, and shalt honor him, not doing thine own ways, nor finding thine own pleasure; nor speaking thine own words:

14. Then shalt thou delight thyself in the Lord, and I will cause thee to ride upon the high places of the earth, and feed thee with the heritage of Jacob thy father: for the mouth of the Lord hath spoken it.

- Deuteronomy 32:7-14 tells about the heritage of Jacob:

7. Remember the days of old, consider the years of many generations: Ask thy father and he will show thee, thy elders, and they will tell thee.

8. When the most High divided to the nations their inheritance, when he separated the sons of Adam, he set the bounds of the people according to the number of the children of Israel.

9. For the Lord's portion is his people; Jacob is the lot of his inheritance,

10. He found him in a desert land, and in the waste howling wilderness; he led him about, he instructed him, he kept him as the apple of his eye.

11. As an eagle stirreth up her nest, fluttereth over her young, spreadeth abroad her wings, taketh them, beareth them on her wings:

12. So the Lord alone did lead him, and there was no strange gods with him.

13. He made him ride on the high places of the earth that he might eat the increase of the fields: and he made them to suck honey out of the rock, and oil out of the flinty rock:

14. Butter of kine, and milk of sheep, with fat of lambs, and rams of the breed of Bashan, and goats, with the fat of the kidneys of wheat; and thou didst drink the pure blood of the grape.

So, fasting is not to get God to answer us, or to show others our ability to go without or to appear "super spiritual", but fasting helps us to tap in to the spiritual, mental and physical benefits God has made available to us:

- Breakthroughs in the spiritual realm, such as revelations and answers to spiritual questions or problems we might have, insight into the true nature of God, and wisdom and understanding of the scriptures.

We put ourselves in position to hear from God. Fasting also helps us to have a crisp, clear awareness of another world: the spirit world.

- In the mental area, fasting also helps you to renew your mind and helps you to become aware of possibilities you may never have thought were within your reach. A renewed mind can literally change your life in all areas: spirit, soul, body, socially and financially, especially when you spend your fasted time ministering to the Lord in thanksgiving, prayer, praise, reading the scriptures, and in studying, meditation and quiet time, (listening to your spirit) as it is in communion with the Spirit of God.

- Just the mention of (the word) fasting can bring many different thoughts to the hearer's mind: such as legalism, drudgery, burden, negative discipline, starvation, discomfort or a variety of other negatives.

But the rewards far out-weigh the negatives, such as: self control, positive discipline, the joy of tapping into the spirit world; a rejuvenation of spirit, soul and body; mastering the 'flesh'; drawing closer to God; receiving healing; preparing yourself for greater ministry; becoming better at work and in all your endeavors; developing the fruit of the spirit; cleansing your physical system; to help break bondages or habits that you, or a loved one may have; receiving divine revelation; the rewards are endless.

Yet you don't have to fast for physical punishment, or for long periods of time to receive rewards. If your motives are right, fasting for one week or one day may very well bring the reward you are seeking. While fasting for 21 days, or 40 days with the wrong motive (or reason) may only bring the rewards of lost weigh, and lost time!

*** My Own Experience Of Fasting ***

Prior to April 12, 1978, I didn't know much, or anything about fasting. I thought it was something very religious people, (like monks), do, or some "super spiritual" person did, but it never occurred to me that it would be something I would ever do, because prior to that time (the day I accepted Jesus as Lord and Savior), I didn't know that I could go a day without food. (They used to call me "Big Bob" at that time), but after surrendering my life to God, I realized that there was another world out there, more real, and more important that this natural, physical world that we live in. I started reading the Bible, and it made sense, before then, it was like an ordinary book. I would read it, but didn't understand what it was saying until my 'eyes' (spiritual eyes) were opened, then I realized I had access to the power of the universe, The Creator of the world; the answer to all the questions and problems of mankind; so, I dug in, I read and I read from cover to cover in several weeks. *This was a new chapter in my life; one I didn't know existed, even though I was raised up in church. Religion is not the way to find God, in fact, religion is designed to keep you away from God. You will never find God through religion!

Christianity is a relationship, not a religion. *Well, back to the subject of fasting: While reading the book of Daniel, I saw where Daniel fasted for ten days, even though it was a partial fast, through a "misunderstanding" of the scriptures, I took it to mean a total fast, (without food), so being led by the fact that this was something I could do, I decided to fast for ten days. This was the beginning of several breakthroughs I have had since becoming a Christian, especially since being in bondage to food (and the unhealthy kind!) was one of my biggest problems.

- I learned that a "foodaholic" can be just as bad as an alcoholic. Sometimes, I remember the days of the fried pork chops and the cheesecake, and the other high fat, high cholesterol foods that were weighing me down (or, up, anyway you look at it!), and the nights I would lie in bed awake because my heart was beating so loud, I couldn't sleep! But, thank God for His mercy!

So, fasting and self-control have played a tremendous role in my life. Being born with a few birth defects, my childhood seemed normal, even though there were some times I felt rejected or my self-esteem was low, there was always 'something' in me that made me think "there is a better world". I believe that is why I day-dreamed a lot back then! I was always caught up in another 'world': I guess it was a way to escape this present evil one!

But, it was during my early adulthood that the real struggles in life began. My physical body was out of shape; I couldn't dress the way I wanted to; I couldn't go to the places I wanted to go; even though I wasn't handicapped physically (It was in my thinking!). So, I struggled in my young adult years, basing everything on the natural, physical, seen world.

- The answer to all my spiritual, mental, physical, social or financial problems was not in the seen world, but in the spiritual, but I didn't know that, so I suffered. I can remember the nightmares, the sleepless nights, the out of body experiences, the fight for my life as alien forces tried to drag my spirit out of my body! Depression is a dangerous and deadly thing, but Thank God for his mercy! It's only through knowing God, that you can know that all things are possible with God.

- Another breakthrough (I would say, the major one) I had through fasting was in the early 80's. I began what I called a 'progression fast' that lasted for 90 days. This one was phenomenal. I had to have had supernatural guidance and help to accomplish that one! I had spiritual opposition, but God and I prevailed.

- At the beginning of the 90 days, I cut out all the sweets: the candies, cookies, cakes, pies, etc. *After about two weeks, out went the other junk such as 'chips' and high fat items. *Then I cut out the diary products, so for several days I ate vegetables, very little meat; starches and juices.

- Then as the last 21 days approached, I was challenged to go on a total fast where I abstained from food and water (I wouldn't recommend anyone to fast for that long without liquids, especially water, since water acts as a cleansing agent for your physical system). Now, I did drink a half glass of water after the tenth day, that was about all I could take.

The amazing thing about the entire 21 days of fasting was that I had no physical problems or discomfort at all.

I believe that it was because of the fact that I had prepared myself weeks before by cutting out the foods that the body craves, like the sweets, starches, etc. *But spiritually, the test, the temptations were trying and somewhat taxing on my mental areas, but God is faithful!

1 Corinthians 10:13

There hath no temptation taken you but such as is common to man: but God is faithful who will not suffer you to be tempted above that you are able, but will with the temptation also make a way to escape, that ye may be able to bear it.

Actually, these test come from the devil, mainly to lead you off into false doctrines or beliefs. Since you become more aware of spiritual things when you are fasting, the enemy disguises himself (as God) to lead you into error where the Word of God is concerned. The devil will do anything to discredit the Word of God, especially when he knows that the Word is real to you, that the spiritual world is real to you, and that both the spiritual and the natural worlds are subject to the Word of God. So God, being faithful, led me through those 90 days victoriously!

One of the first visitors I had, after coming off the fast, looked at me and said, "A miracle!". Previously, I weighed around 220 pounds, and was up there for several years, now I am down to about 150 pounds with a crisp spirit – a renewed mind – and a rejuvenated body!

Fasting does wonders when done properly on the Word of God. Fasting doesn't have to be long and drawn out to get results. I have been on numerous fasts of various durations: 1-day fast; 2 days; 3 days; 4 days; 7 days; 10 days, 14 days and that one time of 21 days, and some of the most rewarding were the 1 day (24 hour) fasts.

Now, lets look at the different kinds of fasts that I have heard of and a brief explanation of each one:

Several Kinds of Fast

1. **Partial Fast**

    This is a period of time when you have restricted yourself from certain foods especially foods that are pleasant to the taste - as in Daniel Chapter One.

2. **A Total Fast**

    Is when you abstain from all solid foods for a period of time - (but not water).

3. **A Supernatural Fast**

    (This should be done only under the leading of God)

    A supernatural fast is abstaining from food and water for a certain time as Moses did in **Exodus 34:28** for forty days - in **Esther 4:15**. Esther requested that the Jews fast for three days (without food or water).

4. **A Juice Fast**

    This type of fast is done by partaking of juices only, no solid food. Some health professionals and nutritionist recommend this type of fasting.

5. **News Fast**

    This type of fasting, I would say, is good for your soul. During a news fast, you abstain from reading or hearing anything in the news.

Fasting

6. A Proclaimed Fast

Is such as when the leader of a nation, church or organization calls for everyone to voluntarily abstain from food for a certain length of time, as in **2 Chronicles 20:3-4.**

7. A Personal Fast

This kind is when you personally set aside a time of abstinence for whatever reason. It may be just to fellowship with God without the influences of the natural or to seek God for the solution to some problems you might have. You decide the length of time, whether partial, total, or juice or whatever. This is the most popular and should be done according to Matthew 6:16-18, and you can be assured of the reward.

How To Fast

Fasting means to abstain, so it can be done simply by abstaining or doing without whatever you decide to refrain from for a set period of time.

Some Guidelines for Fasting

Don't fast without the Word of God. Primarily, fasting should be a time of seeking God.

1. Decide the purpose
2. Proclaim the fast before the Lord and ask for His assistance
3. Believe for the rewards of fasting
4. Minister to the Lord in praise and thanksgiving
5. Prepare yourself to minister to others
6. Expect the angels of God to help you

Spend time in prayer. Pray also in the spirit (in tongues), this is a great way to draw wisdom.

Fasting

Always be aware of God's presence since fasting helps you to be in tuned to the spiritual world, you must know that there are spirits other than God's that would try to lead you. **Deuteronomy 32:12** says there were no strange gods with him. You don't want to be led by strange gods!

The Fasted Life

A most rewarding way of fasting is to live a fasted life: Not going overboard, not just in eating but in every area of life. Never eat all you want, keep your flesh under, especially if there are certain foods you like or seem to be addicted to. Your appetite for certain foods can sometimes rule you! But a 'fasted' way of life helps you to stay disciplined. I've been that way for several years.

I would advise that you take precautions when fasting at work, especially if your work involves physical labor. I would recommend at least one meal during the workday, even though I have fasted for up to five days while working. Fasting should not be to punish your body.

Fasting the news is another way of living a calm, serene life. Not that you are unaware of current events, but you limit the amount of news you hear. You don't need to hear about murder, corruption and high interest rates every day! Get into the Good News (The Bible) or something inspirational or motivational and you may be able to help change some of the bad news!

You don't need to indulge yourself in immoral soap operas or sitcoms when you are seeking God for His help to change a situation or a condition you are in: Remember **Mark 4:24** "take heed what you hear." (Watch what goes into your heart). The cares of this world will choke the Word in your heart and will cause it (the Word) to be non-productive, in other words, you won't see a manifestation of what you have believed for.

CHAPTER SIX

The Power of Meditation

Joshua 1:8

This book of the Law shall not depart out of thy mouth, but thou shalt meditate therein day and night that thou mayest observe to do according to all that is written therein, for then thou shalt make thy way prosperous, and then thou shalt have good success.

Meditation: What is Meditation?

Meditation: to attend to, practice, to ponder, to imagine, to reflect on, to pay attention to, to continue in, to dwell on, to think about, "to talk to yourself"!

Imagine – Imagination – a thought, reasoning, to think over, thoughts and ideas, to care for, "be diligent in", to practice as a result of planning, or devising, to ponder, formation of mental images, to conceive, to form an image of, to reflect, to portray, conceivable, a conception of some event, to represent or picture to oneself, to suppose or think to be, to 'see' beforehand, to mentally imagine, "to play a 'mental' movie in your mind".

Meditation is a major key to success. God, in creating the heavens and the earth, used meditation. He thought beforehand of what he wanted. He had an image of exactly how he wanted the universe to be, and then he spoke that image, and it came to pass exactly the way he wanted it. **Genesis 1:31** – And God saw everything that he had made and behold it was very good.

We are made in the image and likeness of God for a reason. We are not to depend on luck, or chance to fulfill God's calling on our lives. God's Word contains instructions on how we are to function in every area of life. When we go to the Word, read it, believe it, meditate it, and do it, then we are fulfilling God's plan and purpose for us.

Many people, including Christians, say they don't know what their purpose is, or their calling, not realizing that God made us free moral agents with the capacity to dream, imagine, create our own world. However, it should be based on His Word. If it is a particular calling or office, it will be revealed when we are engaged in doing His known will: His Word, (eg – Love the Lord thy God with all thy heart, soul, and mind; Love thy neighbor as thyself; Give and it shall be given unto you, **Luke 6:38**. Pray one for another, **James 5:16**, Work as unto the Lord; Delight thyself also in the Lord, and He shall give thee the desires of thine heart, **Psalm 37:4**). What is in your heart?

God has equipped us to create our own world! God's Word is His will. Is it God's will to heal? **3 John 2**, Beloved, I wish above all things that thou mayest prosper and be in health, even as thy soul prospers. A prosperous soul is a soul that meditates on God's Word.

What Meditation Can Do For You

Here are some of the benefits of Meditation:

- Put you in touch with God, and the supernatural
- Eliminate sickness and disease
- Give you creative ideas
- Reduce stress and anxiety
- Strengthens your immune system
- Lower blood pressure
- Bring freedom from addictive behaviors
- Gain self control
- Bring spiritual maturity
- Helps you to focus your energy on important tasks
- Helps in time management
- Helps you to become the best 'you'
- Expands your opportunities
- Move you ahead in your career
- Increase your confidence
- Build capacity for faith
- Navigate you around life's roadblocks

- Helps you to solve problems
- Helps you to 'see' that all things are possible
- Sharpens your thinking
- Increase your perception
- Improve your memory
- Conquer depression
- Quiets mental conflicts
- Gives you a favorable outlook
- Transform your life
- Give insights
- Give your faith direction
- Helps you to weather any storm
- Keeps you immovable from your dreams
- Makes your way prosperous
- Cause you to have good success
- Cause you to deal wisely in all the affairs of life
- Dramatically change your health and well being
- Better your relationships
- Improve your skills
- Change your way of thinking
- Make you a "No Limit" person
- Build your self-esteem
- Make the incurable, curable
- Cause you to see how to make the unobtainable, obtainable
- Conquer bad habits
- Helps establish good habits
- Enhance your creativity

- Help you make wise decisions
- Improve your problem solving ability
- Help you to relax
- Gain control of your life
- Brings freedom in your life
- Help you set goals
- Helps create an exciting career
- Sharpens your understanding
- Brings hope to a 'hopeless' situation
- Help you to see your purpose
- Give meaning to life
- Give you solid plans
- Brings joy and satisfaction

Faith, Hope and Love are the Keys to Life

1 Corinthians 13:13 - And now abide faith, hope and love, these three, but the greatest of these is love.

Love is the cure of all human ills. (See yourself as a loving person).

Meditation Brings Hope

Hope is vitally important for anyone facing a seemingly 'hopeless' situation. This hope I'm talking about is a supernatural Bible Hope. There are two kinds of hope. (1) Natural Hope is based on the five physical senses, what you see, taste, smell, touch and hear. It falls short of helping someone who faces what medical science calls 'hopeless' or incurable.

(2) Supernatural hope on the other hand is based on the Word of God. Supernatural hope believes in the impossible, it is alive, and when mixed with faith will bring to pass the thing hoped for. Hope operates in the human imagination.

Rom. 15:13 - Now the God of hope fill you with all joy, and peace in believing, that you may abound in hope through the power of the Holy Ghost.

Medical researchers are finding out that the make-up of a person: spirit, soul and body must be in synch in order to keep the healing system operating at its optimal level.

- A sound heart (spirit) is the life of the flesh – (**Proverbs 14:30**). A sound spirit is one that is undisturbed, relaxed and in a tranquil state, (peaceful), producing love, joy, patience, etc. (the fruit of the spirit).

Over 80% of people in the hospitals are there because of conditions that began in their spiritual or emotional area and eventually affected their physical body. A positive, optimistic attitude is conducive to good health.

Affecting a change through meditation

Proverbs 23:7 - For as he thinketh in his heart, so is he. We become what we continually think (meditate) about.

All permanent changes take place on the inside of a person, so by creating positive, healthful images on the inside of you: mentally seeing yourself healed, whole: the way the Word of God describes you, and speaking that image into your spirit. Unseen, power-full forces go to work to bring about the desired results.

In the case of meditating or imaging, see yourself healed or free of a certain sickness, disease or whatever, sometimes viewing pictures of a healthy organ or having an idea of how the internal system operates, especially the immune system, you can focus on a clearer image of the thing desired.

God gave us an imagination: to dream, to imagine, to create, (you can create within yourself a healthy body

Meditation

- Scientists have stated that the average human being operates on only 10-15% of their mental capacity! Since God created man (the human race) in His image, after His likeness, what happened to the other 85%? It is hidden in our imagination! What you can imagine you can be!

Proverbs 23:7 – For as he thinketh in his hearth, so is he!

We become what we think about! What we continually picture or 'see' in our minds eye.

- The first man Adam had the ability to operate at peak performance: 100%, because he had direct contact with the creator, who some call Infinite Intelligence. When he, [Adam] transgressed against God, he lost that ability.

- Adam was wired' to function on a higher level that what we operate on today, so, falling from that position caused everyone born after him to have flaw in the human spirit and thinking ability and eventually in his physical body which allowed the enemy of the soul'; satan, to inject his deception into the mind of man, to change God's original intent for His creation:

Genesis 1:26-28 - And God said, Let us make man in our image, after our likeness: and let them have dominion over the fish of the sea and over the foul of the air, over the cattle and over every creeping thing that creepeth upon the earth.

27.   So God created man in His own image, in the image of God created he him, male and female created He them.

28.   And God BLESSED them, and God said unto them, Be Fruitful, multiply, and replenish the earth and subdue it: and have dominion over the fish of the sea, and over the fowl of the air, and over every living thing that moves upon the earth.

- Since the fall of man, man has gone about to seek his own way:

Genesis 6:5

And God saw that the wickedness of man was great in the earth and that every imagination of the thoughts of his heart was only evil continually.

- They had their own agenda at the Tower of Babel.

Genesis 11:6 - And the Lord said, Behold, the people is one, and this they begin to do, and now nothing will be restrained from them which they imagined to do.

- Our imagination is very powerful!

- We are God like creatures with God-like qualities and abilities. We have the ability to dream, and create.

- Meditation has always been an effective "secret" for success. A study of some of the most successful people in history will reveal the powerful force of meditation as they imagined themselves where they wanted to be, and then followed their imagination. In making the 'incurable', curable or the 'impossible' possible, this powerful tool of meditation is available to everyone, anyone who would dare to dream the impossible. Know that, if thou (you) can believe, all things are possible to him who believes. (**Mark 9:23**).

Meditation is not a mystery, especially when we consider the fact that thousands upon thousands of people use meditation in the negative, (because most of the world is going in a negative flow.) What is negative meditation? Worry!

Worry is basically seeing, or imagining yourself receiving the worst: (being defeated, losing, dying, ashamed, embarrassed, etc.). Worry comes from listening to and looking at natural, physical circumstances that are contrary to our favorable outcome. And by worrying, or imagining the negative, you actually draw those negative conditions into your life! But, if you follow God's plan such as in **Philippians 4:6**: Be careful for nothing (in other words, don't worry about anything) but let your request be made known to God. And then **Philippians 4:8** tells us what to think (or meditate) on: whatsoever things are true, whatsoever things are honest, whatsoever things are just, whatsoever things are pure, whatsoever things are lovely, whatsoever things are of good report, if there be any virtue and if there be any praise, think (or meditate) on these things.

The Word tells us that we must carefully choose what we think about, or dwell on. Meditating on good will override the bad!

How do you Meditate?

There is no one set rule for meditation. A good way is to find a quiet spot or place where you are undisturbed for a few minutes. Close your eyes, take a deep breath, breath out and mentally image or create pictures in your mind of the way you want things to be. The best way is to find a promise in the Bible that covers your particular situation and think about, internalize, visualize, imagine yourself the way that Word describes you, say for instance, you are faced with a physical ailment, your scripture could be

1 Peter 2:24 - By whose stripes ye were healed - you see yourself free from that condition, and the words "ye were healed" giving you the right to see yourself that way. You can mutter to yourself, "I were healed", well, were is past tense, were means I'm already healed, "and picture yourself that way regardless of how you feel, how you look or anything else that's contrary. What will happen is your brain will pick up those images and send signals throughout your body to release chemicals, hormones, etc., to work on the symptoms to bring to pass a picture in your body that matches the imagined one! That is why it is very important to 'kick' worry or imagining vain things.

Remember the old saying, "Be careful what you hope for: you may get it." Things you hope for paint pictures in your mind. Your 'subconscious' or spirit is designed to bring to pass things you continually imagine, speak and believe, good or evil, so, to maintain good health and a sense of well-being in your life, it is imperative that you speak words of healing and health, and have an image on the inside of yourself being in vibrant health continually. Then add the other necessary ingredients, such as living a life of love, a healthy diet and exercise.

Whatever you can imagine, you can be!

Meditation works like this: you imagine a thing in your mind, then you speak that thing into your spirit. By continually speaking, your spirit accepts the image of the thing and goes to work to create or produce an exact copy of the thing imagined (your spirit has creative power - the mind doesn't - that's why it has to go from your mind into your spirit). Your spirit then sends a command back to your mind, where the brain functions and your brain commands your body to line up with the image of the thing imagined, (your immune system and all other systems has to obey the command sent by your spirit!

- Your nervous system doesn't know the difference between a real experience or one imagined, it just responds!

Eg. * Have you ever had a dream where you had to run from a dangerous situation? When you woke up, you noticed you were sweating and your heart was beating rapidly, and while during the whole time you didn't even leave the bed!

- "Meditation rules the World," someone said.

CHAPTER SEVEN

Confession
Brings Possession

Genesis 1:1, 3, 6, 9, 11, 14, 20, 24, 26, 31

1. In the beginning God created the heavens and the earth.

3. And God said, Let there be light; and there was light.

6. And God said, -- v7 – and it was so

9. And God said; -- and it was so

11. And God said; -- and it was so

14. And God said; -- v15 – and it was so

20. And God said; -- v21 – and God saw that it was good

24. And God said; -- and it was so

26. And God said, Let us make man in our image, after our likeness

31. And God saw everything that He had made, and behold, it was very good.

A very important thing to learn from these verses of scripture is that when God speaks, or says something, whatever He says happens, or "it was so." Also, note that after God 'said' something, He saw what He said. He expected what He said to come to pass. Because He saw it on the inside first! Notice **verse 26**: And God said; let us make man in our image after our likeness. And let them have dominion over the fish of the sea, and over the fowl of the air, and over the cattle, and over all the earth and over every creeping thing that creepeth upon the earth. **V27** - So God created man in His own image -----.

We (mankind) are made in the image and likeness of God. When we speak, we should expect it (what we speak) "to be so.".

As creatures made in the image and likeness of God we should expect to see what we say. (God said, and He saw).

We shouldn't take our words lightly. We create things, (good or bad), with our words! (By our confessions)

Matthew 12:35-37

35.   A good man out of the good treasure of the heart brings forth good things: And an evil man out of the evil treasure brings forth evil things.

36.   But I say unto you, That for every idle word that men shall speak, They shall give account thereof in the day of judgment.

37.   For by thy words thou shalt be justified, and by thy words, thou shalt be condemned.

God is placing a high value on your words! Why? It is because words have creative power. Words can create and words can destroy!

Lets Define Confess - Confession

Confession – The declaration of the acts of God by which man is rescued from his troubles, A proclamation, to declare, to call upon, to acknowledge, to tell or to make known, to declare faith in or adherence to. To profess, to give evidence of, admit, own, affirm, to claim.

When we are confessing, we are actually declaring, admitting, owning, affirming and claiming what we are saying!

We shouldn't look at the word confess or confession as much in the negative sense (such as confessing sin) as we do in the positive.

Hebrews 3:1 - Wherefore, holy brethren, partakers of the heavenly calling, consider the apostle and High Priest of our profession (or confession) Christ Jesus.

Jesus is the High Priest of our Words! He works for us, and in our behalf according to our words. We shouldn't take our words lightly. Your words can close the doors or your words can open doors. Your words create your (life) world.

Watch your words! Your words shape your life! Words can make us or break us. Words can heal us, or make us sick!

When you are confessing words, you are calling for whatever those words describe: For instance, if you say "I am sick" (now you may be experiencing or having some lying symptoms). By saying or continually saying "I am sick," you are calling forth sickness. So to counter that, you should say: "I refuse this feeling or these symptoms in my body! "By the stripes of Jesus I am healed."

We must train ourselves to say only what we want. **Joel 3:10b** says, Let the weak say, "I am strong." In **Romans 4:17;** we see Abraham following God, in calling those things which be not as though they were. We are made in the image and likeness of God, and we are to speak into existence what we desire. Jesus said you shall have whatsoever you say. We have been trained by negative forces, such as religion, to speak negative things. Our words can entrap us! We are judged by our words, **Matthew 12:37**.

We need to be aware at all times that unseen agents are awaiting our words. When we speak positive words, agents of God go to work to make our words good or bring our words to pass. However, by speaking or confessing negative words, the agents of darkness, of the negative world go to work to bring those negative things you speak into manifestation.

Proverbs 18:21 says that, death and life are in the power of the tongue. When you speak, you speak words of life or words of death.

Our confessions rule us! Confessions bring possessions, good or bad (evil). That brings to my mind how that just confessing Jesus as Lord brought about a life changing experience in my life.

Romans 10:9-10 - That if thou shalt confess with thy mouth the Lord Jesus, and shalt believe in thine heart that God hath raised Him from the dead, thou shalt be saved. For with the heart man believeth unto righteousness, and with the mouth confession is made unto salvation.

I was thrilled at the fact that just confessing, "God forgive me of my sins, Jesus, I receive you now as my Lord and my savior," my whole life was transformed from a world of darkness into a world of light that is very much alive!

What you constantly confess, you will eventually believe, what you consistently believe, you will eventually receive. Words bring things to pass.

Hebrews 11:3 - says that by faith God spoke substances into existence. Faith's results are determined by your confession.

Another definition of confession means to acknowledge faith in, or to acknowledge or own-up to. So when you are confessing, you are subconsciously saying, "I believe in what I am saying," (whether it is good or evil, constructive or destructive)!

Do you 'see' what you are saying when you say something like "O, this headache is killing me"?

Don't say anything you don't want. Speak only words that God can act on.

What is Confession

1. Confession is stating something we believe

2. Confession is declaring something we know to be true

3. Confession is proclaiming a truth we have accepted wholeheartedly

You must realize also that, what you say is more important (or just as important) than what you believe, Why? I just stated the fact that agents act on words. We have an enemy, the devil, and he knows that if he can't defeat us with words, he can't defeat us.

So he brings trials, temptations, test, or the like against us to get us to speak (or confess) the adverse situation. And so, by speaking what you see, or feel, you are perpetuating your own problem! Instead, when we are faced with a trial, or whatever is against us, we need to know what God's Word says; and think and speak only in line with God's Word.

We must remember that our confessions rule us. So let your word - All of your words, work for you instead of against you. When you get up in the morning, you should arise with positive confessions on your lips, "I love you, Lord, with all my heart, with all my soul, and with all my mind, and with all my strength, and my neighbor as myself." (Remember, Love is the cure of all human ills!)

Jesus and Confession

Jesus the High Priest of our profession (confession) (**Hebrews 3:1**) was constantly confessing who He was; His mission; and where He was from.

In **Luke 4:18-21** - The Spirit of the Lord is upon me, because He hath anointed me to preach the gospel to the poor: He hath sent me to heal the brokenhearted, to preach deliverance to the captives, and recovering of sight to the blind; To set at liberty them that are bruised, to preach the acceptable year of the Lord. And he closed the book and gave it again to the minister, and sat down. And the eyes of all them that were in the synagogue were fastened on Him. And He began to say unto them, this day is this scripture fulfilled in your ears.

Jesus was saying, "I am the One this scripture is talking about"!

More of His Confessions

"I am not come to destroy"

"I am meek and lowly in heart"

"I, the Son of man, am –

"Is your eye evil because "I am good"?

"I am able"

"I am with you always"

"I am among you as him that serves"

"I am he" [the MESSIAH]

"I am the bread of Life"

"I am the Living bread"

"I know Him [The Father], for I am from Him"

"I am the Light of the World" **John 8:12**"

"I am not of this world"

"I am the door"

"I am come that they might have life"

"I am the way, the truth, and the life"

"I am the resurrection and the life"

"I am in the Father and He in me"

"I am the true vine" **John 15:1**

"I am not alone"

"I am from above"

Now that you have heard some of Jesus' confessions, what are you going to confess about yourself?

What do you confess about yourself?

When you are going through a tough situation, or facing hard times – this is a good time! -- To check up on your confessions. Listen to what you are saying. Without a doubt, your negative confessions are perpetuating your problems. I remember going through a trial several years ago. My biggest problem was my tongue. Contrary circumstances would present themselves, and instead of keeping a positive confession on the Word of God, I was responding to the circumstances, and this went on for almost two years, until finally after being frustrated enough, I was listening to a guest pastor at church one night talking about faith and confessions. He said, "when you are standing on a promise of God, you latch on to that promise like a bulldog," (and don't let go until it is manifested). Then he asked the question: How do you let go? -- (before it's manifested), then he pointed at his tongue. When he did that I almost jumped out of my chair! I caught it as a revelation, and when I did, the Lord spoke to me and said; "That won't happen to you again". Well, things didn't change (in the natural) overnight, but I was on my way out!

Now looking back at some major events in my past, I can 'see' how my confessions played a vital role in bringing things to pass, positive and negative.

Proverbs 6:2 - Thou art snared with the words of thy mouth, thou art taken with the words of thy mouth.

Listen to yourself sometimes (while you are talking) especially about what you are saying about yourself. We listen to others sometimes more than we listen to ourselves. Not realizing that you will believe 'you' (yourself) more than you would believe anyone else. For instance, someone says to you: "You can't do that" but you reply: "O, yes I can" - you believe you! Now, if you let that person persuade you into believing you can't and you agree with them: you won't! But you don't have to agree with anybody's negative opinion of you. Boldly confess I can do all things through Christ who strengthens me!

What should you confess about yourself? You should confess what God says about you. You are today what you have been confessing yesterday, or in the past.

What do we confess as believers?

#1. What God did for us through Christ in His plan of Redemption -- Colossians 1:13 - who hath delivered us from the power of darkness and hath translated us into the kingdom of his dear son.

"I've been delivered from the power of darkness, translated into the kingdom of God's dear Son, in whom I have redemption through His blood."

#2. What God has done in us by the Word and the Holy Ghost.

2 Corinthians 5:17 - Therefore if any man be in Christ, he is a new creature, old things are past away, behold all things are become new.

"I am a new creature in Christ Jesus."

2 Peter 1:3, 5 - According as his divine power hath given unto us all things that pertain to life and godliness, through the knowledge of him that hath called us to glory and virtue, whereby are given unto us (me) exceeding great and precious promises:

5. - And besides this, giving all diligence, add to your faith virtue, and to virtue knowledge, and to knowledge temperance, and to temperance patience, and to patience godliness and to godliness, brotherly kindness, and to brotherly kindness, charity (love). For if these things be in you and abound, they make you that ye shall neither be barren nor unfruitful in the knowledge of our Lord Jesus Christ. "I am a new creature in Christ Jesus."

#3. Confess who we are to God in Christ Jesus - **Ephesians 2:10** - For we are his workmanship, created in Christ Jesus. "I am his workmanship "created in" Christ Jesus

#4. What Jesus is presently doing for us at the right hand of the Father - **Hebrews 3:1** - Wherefore holy brethren, partakers of the heavenly calling, consider the apostle and high priest of our profession (confession): Christ Jesus. "It is my apostle and High Priest, my intercessor, my Lord, my Advocate."

#5. What the Word can accomplish in us as we confess it - **Acts 20:32** - And now brethren, I commend you to God, and to the Word of His grace, which is able to build you up, and give you an inheritance among them which are sanctified.

We are to make our confessions based on the Word of God, and hold fast (stick) to our confessions.

Here is a list of my personal "I am" confessions; make these your daily confessions

"I AM"

"I am a champion" (Daniel 11:32)

"I am successful" (Joshua 1:8)

"I am prosperous" I am strong" I am courageous (Joshua 1:8, 9)

"I am an achiever" (Psalm 1)

"I am a winner" (Philippians 3:8)

"I am more than a conqueror" (Romans 8:37)

"I am a rich man" (2 Corinthians 8:9)

"I am a wealthy man" (Deuteronomy 8:18)

"I am a spirit, I have a soul, I live in a physical body" (1 Thessalonians 5:23)

"I am a new creature in Christ Jesus" (2 Corinthians 5:17)

"I am the redeemed of the Lord" (Galatians 3:13 - Colossians 1:13)

"I am delivered from the power of darkness" (Colossians 1:13)

"I am translated into the kingdom of God's dear Son (in whom I have redemption through His blood) (Colossians 1:13)

"I am the righteousness of God in Christ Jesus" (2 Corinthians 5:21)

"I am an heir of God, I am a joint heir with Jesus Christ" (Romans 8:17)

"I am saved" (Romans 10:13)

"I am free"

"I am sanctified" (1 Thessalonians 5:23)

"I am holy"

"I am whole"

"I am forgiven" "I am forgiving", "I am a forgiver"

"I am healed" (1 Peter 2:24)

"I am alive unto God"

"I am gentle"

"I am bold"

"I am victorious"

"I am wise"

"I am a king"

"I am a priest"

"I am a family man"

"I am faithful"

"I am full of faith"

"I am a covenant man"

"I am established"

"I am appreciative"

'I am thankful"

"I am a son of God" (1 John 3)

"I am the head and not the tail" (Deuteronomy 28)

"I am above only and not beneath" (Deuteronomy 28)

"I am indwelt by the Greater one - (greater is He that is in me, than he that
  is in the world")

"I am friendly" "I am kind"

"I am debt-free"

"I am assured"

'I am a living stone"

"I am a believer"

"I am seated with Christ"

"I am the handiwork of God"

"I am fully persuaded"

"I am blessed in the city"

"I am blessed in the field"

"I am I am blessed" "I am sound"

"I am joyful"

"I am protected"

"I am kept"

"I am receptive"

"I am confident"

"I am filled with knowledge"

"I am sober"

"I am aware"

"I am vigilant"

"I am mature"

"I am an intercessor"

"I am understanding"

"I am a builder"

"I am the light of the world"

"I am honest"

"I am steadfast"

"I am diligent"

"I am unmovable"

I am abounding:

"I am abounding in faith"

"I am abounding in hope"

"I am abounding in love"

"I am abounding in knowledge"

"I am willing" (Isaiah 1:19)

"I am obedient" (Isaiah 1:19)

"I am skillful in all learning and wisdom" (Daniel 1:17)

"I am gracious"

"I am worthy" (Ephesians 4:1)

"I am supplied" (Philippians 4:19)

"I am sure"

"I am innocent"

"I am clean"

"I am helped"

"I am fearfully and wonderfully made"

"I am pure"

'I am prudent"

"I am the Lord's"

"I am filled with Power"

"I am powerful"

"I am able"

"I am glad"

"I am filled with comfort"

"I am full"

"I am peaceful"

"I am good"

"I am triumphant"

"I am in Him"

"I am called"

"I am predestined" (Ephesians 1:5)

"I am justified"

"I am anointed"

"I am glorified"

"I am accepted in the beloved"

"I am blessed and highly favored"

"I am Love" (See: The Law of the Spirit of life -- Love is)

"I am the temple of the Holy Ghost"

"I am chosen"

"I am blameless"

"I am in Christ"

Another Example:

Deuteronomy 28:27 - The Lord shall smite thee with the botch of Egypt, (the boils of Egypt) and with the emerods, and with the scab (skin diseases) and with the itch, where of thou canst not be healed.

Let's say you have a skin disease - your confession would be like this:

According to **Deuteronomy 28:27**, scab (or skin disease) is a curse of the Law, but according to Galatians 3:13, Christ hath redeemed me from the curse of the Law, Therefore I'm redeemed from skin disease. I call skin disease gone from my body in Jesus Name! I no longer have skin disease, I'm redeemed".

Deuteronomy 28:61 says, also every sickness, and every plague (disease) which is not written in the book of this law, them will the Lord bring upon thee until thou be destroyed.

We can conclude that every sickness and every disease is a curse of the Law. But Christ hath redeemed us from the curse of the law. So, whatever the sickness, disease or condition might be, you can make your confessions based on **Deuteronomy 28:61**.

Healing Scriptures/ Healing Confessions

"According to Deuteronomy 28:15-61: (_Name the condition_) is a curse of the Law. Galatians 3:13 says, Christ hath redeemed me from the curse of the Law, being made a curse for me, Therefore I'm redeemed from _____. I forbid _____to operate in my body. Every sickness, every disease is a curse of the Law. Christ hath redeemed me from the curse of the Law, therefore I'm redeemed from every sickness and every disease. I have a sound body, a normal body, a redeemed body, a free body, free from sickness, disease, infections, virus, fungus, allergies and pain."

"Body, I call you normal, well, whole and free from sickness and disease. Every organ, every muscle, every bone, every joint, every gland, every cell, every tissue, every tooth functions in perfection" "My gum: I have a healthy gum. My eyes: I have perfect vision; My ears: I have perfect hearing; my urinary tract is clear, well and in perfect health. My respiratory system is clear, normal and in perfect health. My eyes are well, whole and function properly. I am healed, well, whole, "Thank you Lord for Divine Health."

My immune system is activated and balanced. My immune system is strong, normal and functions properly. I command my immune system to rise up and attack every foreign invader that has come against my body. Every disease germ, every bad bacteria, every abnormal cell, every bad fungus, every virus: every foreign invader, "My immune system rise up! and attack, drive out, eradicate, eliminate, dissolve and DESTROY you in JESUS NAME!" "I am healed, I am whole", I am well.

NOTE: We are making our confessions by faith, (faith is the substance of things hoped for, the evidence of things not seen) so it is perfectly scriptural to call those things that be not as though they were. Even when I don't feel healed or see healing, Faith says I have it: By His stripes ye (I am) were healed. In **Romans 4:17,** we see Abraham, following God in calling those things which be not as though they were. And even though he and his wife Sarah were childless, he kept calling (confessing) for twenty-five years until his son Isaac was born.

You see the name Abraham meant a father of nations. How could he be a father of nations when he didn't have any offspring? Every time he heard his name called or every time he told someone his name, he had an image of a son being born to him!

Now, every time you confess what you desire, you should have an image of what you are confessing. You say it until you see it. Look at the creation story in **Genesis 1:3-31** -- God said, and he saw!

Now, you say (or confess) these healing scriptures and confessions until you 'see' what you are saying.

*Jesus is the Lord of my life, sickness and disease will not Lord it over   me, I'm redeemed" (Romans 10:9-10)

* "I forgive others as Christ has forgiven me. I'm free from strife and unforgiveness. The love of God rules in my heart." (Mark 11:25)

* "Jesus bore my sins, sickness, disease and pain in His body on the cross, therefore my body is off limits to sin, sickness, disease and pain" (1 Peter 2:24)

* "I am dead to sin and live unto God. I am healed, well and whole." (1 Peter 2:24)

* "According to the Word of God, I am a world overcomer. I overcome the world, the flesh and the devil by the blood of the Lamb and by the word of my testimony" (Revelations 12:11) (1 John 4:4) (1 Peter 5:4-5)

* "God sent His Word and healed me, and delivered me from my destructions." (Psalm 107:20)

* "Through the Word of God, I receive abundant life. This life flow throughout my entire being: spirit, soul and body. I have radiant health!" (John 10:10)

* "As I attend to God's Word, hearken to and obey His voice, they (God's Word) are life, healing and health to all my flesh" (Proverbs 4:20-22)

* "God's Word is medicine to my whole body, "from the crown of my head to the soles of my feet, I am well!" (Proverbs 4:22)

* "According to Psalm 91, no evil shall befall me, no plague come near my dwelling. The angels of God go with me, before me, and they are all around me, I'm protected." (Psalm 91, Hebrews 1:14)

* "My body is the temple of the Holy Ghost, my body is in perfect chemical balance, my blood sugar is normal, my total blood cholesterol is (e,g.) 180, my blood pressure is normal." (1 Corinthians 6:19 -- Mark 11:23).

* "I have been delivered from the power of darkness. The light of God's Word destroys growth, tumors and abnormal cells and restores vibrant health and strength" "I am strong" (Colossians 1:12)

* "The Law of the Spirit of Life in Christ Jesus has made me free from the law of sin and death. The life of God energizes and strengthens every cell of my body." (Romans 8:2)

* "God has not given me the spirit of fear but of power, and of love and of a sound mind. The love of God within me drives out all fear, sickness and oppression." (2 Timothy 1:7) (1 John 4:18)

* "The life of God is in my blood, my blood is clean, pure, and flowing freely."

* "I have a strong heart, every heart beat is normal and functions in perfection."

* "I speak to every bone and every joint in my body, I call you normal, well, whole, free from disease, arthritis, rheumatism, and pain. The healing word of God permeates every bone and joint of my body" Every bone and joint functions in perfection."

* "Bless the Lord, O my soul, and forget not all His benefits: He forgives all my iniquities, He heals all my diseases, He redeemed my life from destruction, He has crowned me with loving kindness and tender mercies, He satisfies my mouth with good things, and my youth is renewed as the eagle's." (Psalm 103:2-5)

* "I will not die, but live, and declare the works of God." (Psalm 118:17)

* "I am blessed coming in and I'm blessed going out, I am the head and not the tail, above only, and not beneath. My enemies are smitten before my face." (Deuteronomy 28:1-13)

A Personal Testimony on Confessions

A few years ago, on the job I was on, we had a health screening (this company had a great program of promoting health, with cash rewards and other incentives). Well, the screening was done in January; (right after all the holiday indulgences!) my blood pressure was 148/90 (higher than normal). My total blood cholesterol registered 232 (normal is 200 or below). The nurse told me my blood sugar was low. Knowing some things about confessions; that confessions brings possession, I went to work on my confessions.

In the meantime I had visited a doctor who told me that he didn't know of any alternative remedy for high cholesterol, and then wrote me out a prescription for (a high cholesterol medication), well I refused the prescription and told him that I would use alternative means to lower my cholesterol level. So, I began to exercise regularly, watch my diet for high fat, high cholesterol foods, most importantly, I watched my confessions - I wrote on a 3x5 card:

"My blood pressure is 120/80"

"My total blood cholesterol is 200 or below"

"My blood sugar is normal"

Those were some of my daily confessions for the next five or so months. When the nurses came back for a screening six months later, the nurse who went over my chart was surprised at the results. She asked me if I were on medication, I told her no. Well, my blood pressure was 120/80, my blood sugar level was normal, and my total blood cholesterol was 188 - confessions bring possessions!

Never Again! Confess:

* Never again confess: satan's supremacy over you - (**Luke 10:19**)

Behold I give you power to tread on serpents and scorpions and over all the power of the enemy.

* Confess: "I'm redeemed by the blood of Jesus. I have been delivered from the power of darkness" (**Colossians 1:13**)

* Never again confess: I'm "weak"

* Confess: (**Psalm 27**) - The Lord is the strength of my life. Let the weak say I am strong. (**Joel 3:10**).

* Never say "I can't".

* Say: I can do all things through Christ which strengthens me.

(**Philippians 4:13**)

* Never say "I am sick"

* Say: By whose stripes "I am healed." (**1st Peter 2:24**)

* Never say things you don't want ("seems like I'm catching a cold")

* Confess only what you do want.

Never Again:

Put yourself down: You are a royal priesthood, a holy nation, a peculiar person, a king and a priest unto God, more than a conqueror, redeemed, healed, free.

Never again continually confess what you don't want, because Jesus said in **Mark 11:23**, you shall have whatsoever you say. If you continually confess what you don't want, you will have what you don't want!

Chapter Eight

Zeroing in On Health and Healing

"Full Speed – Like Nobody's Business"

** Feel Good about Yourself

Imagine yourself the way you want to be: (Healed, Successful, Joyful - prosperous, rich, popular, etc., all day long, every waking moment (regardless of the circumstances). Play a "mental movie" every waking moment of yourself healed, healthy and enjoying life, helping someone else to become!

Confession Brings Possession

"By His stripes, I am healed" confess continually, all day long until something (healing power) spiritual and physical is manifested, (e.g.) say, according to **Deuteronomy 28:15-61** - skin disease (or whatever ailment) is a curse of the law, Christ hath redeemed me from the curse of the law (**Galatians 3:13**) therefore, I no longer have skin disease, I'm redeemed."

PRAISE STOPS THE ENEMY – Psalm 8 – Psalm 9

(See Praise, Thanksgiving and Worship)

Pray without Ceasing – (Example of 24 Hour Group Intercession)

Upon hearing of a member who had a life threatening condition, a particular church prayer group got together and formed a 24 hour intercessory prayer band for the healing and deliverance of that person. In 24 to 48 hours that church member was completely healed. This type of zeroing "in" takes dedication and commitment, but it does produce amazing results when done in faith based on the Word.

Acts 12:5 - Peter therefore was kept in prison: but prayer was made without ceasing of the church unto God for him.

Steps To Receive Healing

#1. Use the Name of Jesus against the devil. Demand in the name of Jesus that the disease and sickness leave. (You must have a good knowledge of the Word of God, especially healing scriptures. Know beyond a shadow of a doubt that healing belongs to you.

Philippians 2:9-11 - Wherefore God also hath highly exalted Him, and given Him a name which is above every name.

10. That at the name of Jesus, every knee should bow, of things (beings) in heaven and things (beings) in earth, and things (beings) under the earth.

11. And that every tongue should confess that Jesus Christ is Lord, to the glory of God the Father.

#2. Pray for healing to the Father in Jesus Name.

John 16:23 - Whatsoever you shall ask the Father in my name, He will give it you.

#3. Agree in Prayer.

Matthew 18:19-20 - Again I say unto you, that if two of you shall agree on earth as touching anything they shall ask, it shall be done for them of my Father which is in heaven. For where two or three are gathered together in my name, there am I in the midst of them.

#4. Anoint with Oil

James 5:14-16 - Is any sick among you? Let him call for the elders of the church, and let them pray for him, anointing him with oil in the name of the Lord, and the prayer of faith shall save the sick, and the Lord shall raise him up, and if he has committed sins, they shall be forgiven him.

16. Confess your faults one to another and pray one for another that ye may be healed. The effectual, fervent prayer of a righteous man availeth much.

- **Note:** The sick person is to call for the elders of the church. Make sure they are Holy Spirit filled Elders who believe in healing.

#5. Receive Healing through the Laying on of hands.

Mark 16:17-18 – And these signs shall follow them that believe: In my name shall they cast out devils ---

18 – They shall lay hands on the sick and they shall recover.

Just the laying on of hands won't heal a person, the laying on of hands act as a 'point of contact' to release your faith. When hands are laid on you, believe that you receive then (regardless of how you 'feel' or what you 'see').

#6. Receive healing through the gifts of healing.

1 Corinthians 12:7-11 - But the manifestation of the Spirit is given to every man to profit withal.

8. For to one is given by the Spirit the Word of Wisdom, to another the Word of Knowledge by the same Spirit.

9. To another faith by the same Spirit; To another the gifts of healing by the same Spirit.

10. To another the working of miracles, to another prophecy, to another discerning of spirits, to another divers kinds of tongues, to another the interpretation of tongues.

The Spiritual gifts were placed in the church by God. These gifts are supernatural manifestations of the Holy Spirit ministering healing power through an anointed minister to individuals. All of the other gifts can also be in operation to set a person free.

The gifts of the Spirit operates as the Spirit wills, and are not always in manifestation; but these gifts are more likely to manifest where the gifts are taught and received, and where there is an atmosphere of expectancy; however faith in the Word of God always work.

7. Know that Healing belongs to you.

The best way or method you can be healed is to know for yourself from the scriptures. **Isaiah 53:4,5, Matthew 8:17** and **1 Peter 2:24** and numerous other scriptures on healing (See Healing Scriptures). Healing is as much a part of our redemption as salvation is. Healing belongs to you.

Note: Sometimes healing comes by degrees, not all the time instantly. So continue to listen to healing scriptures and hold on to your confession of healing; don't be moved by how you feel or any other natural circumstances once you have prayed, or have been prayed for or have had hands laid on you, or any other method for healing has been applied. Receive by faith. Faith comes by hearing and hearing by the Word of God.

You Can Initiate Your Own Miracle

Matthew 17:20 - If you have faith, nothing shall be impossible unto you.

Mark 9:23 - Jesus said unto him, if thou canst believe, all things are possible to him that believeth.

Hebrews 4:12-13 - For the Word of God is quick, (a living thing) (full of living power) full of power to make alive and powerful, (active) (effective), and sharper than any two-edged sword, piercing even to the dividing asunder of soul and spirit, and of the joints and marrow, and is a discerner of the thoughts and intents of the heart. Neither is there any creature that is not manifest in His sight. But all things are naked and open unto the eye of him with whom we have to do.

The Word of God can effectively reach a person in a coma and bring them out. The Word can reach a brain damaged person and bring complete recovery. The Word was made flesh, and dwelt among us. **John 1:14**.

The Word of God is a living thing and will bring life to any lifeless situation. It is of vital importance to "feed," pump the Word of God into a person who has been sick for some time, a paralyzed person or anyone who has been diagnosed as incurable.

Enforce the Word of God in your life by continually confessing, reading - meditating, (picturing-imaging) and speaking. "I am healed", "I am a disease free individual". "Jesus, himself took my infirmities and bore my sicknesses and by his stripes I am healed!" "I have a diseased free body."

Five areas to persist in to bring about a manifestation of healing or anything you are believing God for:

1. Pray in the Spirit - **Jude20-21**

2. Call things which be not as though they were - **Romans 4:17 (I am   healed)**

3. Continual Praise - **Hebrews 13:15**

4. Forgive everyone - **Mark 11:25**

5. Let peace rule in your heart - **Philippians 4:6**

    ** Live Right, Live the love life

    ** Eat Right

    ** Love one another

    ** Exercise Regularly, Stay active

    ** Let Love rule!

Love Never Fails!